THE TRANSUB

BOOK 5: AWAMS REFUGEE

XAVIER THERG

THE TRANSUB

BOOK 5: AWAMS REFUGEE

XAVIER THERG

Published by AOIX Press,
An imprint of White Media Works
San Diego, California

ISBN 978-1-64145-006-5

www.xaviertherg.wordpress.com

Other Works by Xavier Therg

The Bio-Mech War
An existential war between biologicals and mechs.

1: Orphan Rangers	12: Black Claw
2: Clone Pods	13: Hard Landing
3: Space Turtles	14: Smiley War
4: Teardrop Bottles	15: Nowhere Man
5: Blue Iguanas	16: Dawn Fire
6: Crabb World	17: Laughing Boar
7: Big Teeth	18: Lost Cohort
8: Lightning Moths	19: Gray World
9: Galactic Xoo	20: Polychrome
10: Orange Crush	21: Gold Spinner
11: Iron Termites	22: Fusiform

The Transub
The resurrection of humankind
inside quantum portals.

1: Proxima	7: Recall Plateau
2: Q-Port System	8: Lost and Found
3: Algae War	9: Breakup Islands
4: Q-Port Spider	10: Q-Port Makers
5: Awams Refugee	11: Fire Gods
6: Spegellandet	12: Lightship Deicide

Two Worlds Undone
In the tradition of *Beowulf*, the survival of two
worlds is threatened by an open gate between.

1: The Prince	9: The Mayor
2: The Wizard	10: The Rassan
3: The Dolphin	11: The Rill
4: The Wolf Queen	12: The Teacher
5: The King	13: The City
6: The Trog	14: The Breakup
7: The Overtrog	15: The Dragons
8: The Sea Dragon	

Table of Contents

Part 1: Awams

Part 2: Refugee

Excerpt from Book 6: Spegellandet

Part 1 – Awams

Episode 1 – The Factory

It took only nineteen years for the species of human/insect mutants known as the Host to spread to every country in the world. Escaped originally from an abandoned genetics laboratory, the Host established hives like patches of weeds in the grassy field of humanity. When hives reached critical mass they expelled Host queens, seeding new colonies until all the world was infected.

The voracious Host consumed both plants and animals, storing digested paste in underground food banks. How many humans ended their lives in those dark tunnels would never be counted. After the Host, such statistics were meaningless. Humans fought and died in a war that was never even acknowledged by the enemy. The Host followed no cause, no plan, no leader. Stag, bee, termite, ladybug, firefly, mantis, queen: each played a role, giving their lives for the hive.

Humans fought back valiantly, holding a city or town, but for every Host killed, a dozen more crawled from the birthing creches. Human enclaves could hold out for only so long before being absorbed into the patient mass of the Host. Almost too late, humans realized that if they were to survive as a species they would need a champion.

The mechanical impaler crashed through underbrush on six steel legs. Next to a trail the impaler cocked its legs on springs and lowered its camouflaged green and brown platform nearly to the ground. Around the platform's sides and dotted over the surface of a hinged scoop, the impaler had dozens of sharpened blades. Except for a single motion sensor the impaler powered down, content to wait an hour, a day, a week, a month.

A meter and a half tall, naked, and with a white horn protruding from his forehead, the little Host stag would never be confused with a human, but as he scurried along the river trail foraging for berries, he spoke to himself in short worried human whispers, "Find food, hurry, hurry. Queen hungers, find food. Hurry, hurry..."

If they had ever been tested, the highest Host I.Q. on the human scale would have measured in the eighties. The Host conquered not with intelligence but with relntless numbers. They were fearless, and most were armed to some extent. Even a stag, the lowly workman of the hive could stab with the sharp horn on his head.

The stag carried so many berries in his arms they started to fall. He crammed some in his mouth. With his chin dripping red juices, the stag turned for home. He followed the river with short nervous steps, watching across the water for signs of other Host. Lately a neighboring hive had been sending warriors to expand their territory, very troubling. His queen would produce more warriors too but she needed food. The thought drove the little stag's legs even faster. "Queen hungers, hurry, hurry..."

When the impaler flew from the bushes, it happened too fast for the stag to comprehend. Like the sharpened jaws of a bear trap, a daggered scoop flipped down, catching the stag's head and arm. Only when berry juice poured from the stag's mouth did he realize he was in trouble. With his free hand the stag clawed at the scoop. Pinned on top of the platform he wiggled back and forth, trying to get his feet on the ground.

The impaler squeezed with the scoop and raised two steel legs to keep the stag's fleshy legs in the air. In a looping crawl, the impaler worked free of the bushes and headed south along the trail. Motion sensors indicated that the Host was still alive. The stag's squeal indicated a summons for help.

The impaler radioed for instructions. As the Host's thrashing grew weaker, the impaler lowered the side of the platform and scuttled more naturally on all six legs. Following the trail, the impaler crawled through a low grass meadow dragging the Host's limp body behind.

The stag's abduction had not been unobserved. With a fluttering buzz of wings, flying Host dropped out of the air. Like dolls with wings, a Host bee by itself would not be a problem, but one after another they darted in, pulling at the heavy platform. The impaler spun its legs and swung the scoop like a club.

In jerks and slides, the whole buzzing party dragged closer to the river. With no hint of panic the impaler again radioed its position and situation. When the response came back, the impaler tilted its platform, letting the dead stag fall to the ground.

Ignoring the body, the bees continued to harass the impaler, dragging it slowly to the water.

Two kilometers from the sight of the battle, the propeller of a small plane cut the forest silence with a mechanical whine. No living operator on board, the plane pulled onto a narrow strip and buzzed down a twenty meter runway. At the edge of the building the plane lifted off and banked high to clear the tops of pine and maple trees.

Speeding north over the forest, the plane needed no sighting pass. It had no optical sensors in any case. Calculating positions with GPS and flight speed, the plane opened its hatch, letting fall metal ballbearings on a precise vector.

Spreading out in a heavy silver rain, ballbearings pulverized three bees. Half under the platform the fourth bee was only grazed. It limped across the grass and flew off before the impaler could catch it. The impaler crawled back to scoop up the dead stag.

A second impaler appeared in the meadow with a smaller six-legged machine on its back. While the second impaler gathered bees, the carryall climbed down and collected ballbearings in steel claws. It dropped them into a bin in the top of its shell, and then the victorious war machines headed home.

Situated in a forest clearing, the massive factory building was one hundred meters long, fifty meters wide, and three stories tall. First to arrive, the plane landed on one of the rooftop runways. Passing a row of stacks belching smoke, it taxied to a ballbearing chute for a refill. Then it rolled to its hangar and plugged into a battery charger.

An impaler arrived next, crawling to a series of low bins. With the swinging hinge, the stag body was scraped off onto a chute, and carried inside on a belt. The impaler crawled around to the other side of the building for maintenance and a battery exchange before being sent out again to lay in wait for prey. The second impaler dumped its bees into the biomass bins and headed straight to storage.

The carryall came last. Struggling with the heavy load of bearings it climbed a ramp to the roof and transferred bearings from its bin to the plane refiller. When the carryall finished, it climbed to the ground and headed for the garage. A garbage truck needed a complete engine overhaul. The carryall would work through the night.

Monitoring every step with vast arrays of sensors, the factory's complex logic controller wasn't satisfied. In circuits throughout the factory, the self-teaching controller noted inefficiencies. The last bee could have been killed with a second bearing drop, the carryall could have ridden an impaler back, and the first impaler could have collected all four bodies without assistance.

Algorithms would be rewritten to take advantage. Nevertheless, inside the biomass converter, the stag and three bees would produce eighty-four Watt equivalents of power. The energy expenditure by two impalers, plane, and carryall was only sixty-four. A surplus of twenty Watt equivalents could be used to help build the next factory.

Amandacine sat alone in the small room she shared with her father. Two meters wide, and two meters long, the walls barely contained two fold-down bunk beds and fold-out table where Amandacine and her father sometimes ate their meals. Late in the afternoon most of the children played in the town square. Amandacine preferred sitting alone on the top bunk wearing her V-style audio/optical cradle. Covering ears and eyes, the headset transported her to a world not bound by narrow metal walls.

Amandacine was a princess in a world of her own creation called Talon. She rode a flying dragon. Her mother was still alive, although always away on trips to foreign lands. If Amandacine could just kill enough trogs, her mother would come back and rule as Queen of Talon again. Amandacine's father knocked on her head. "Hey, pumpkin."

She had already seen him, dehazing the eye cups when she felt movement in the room. She pulled off the cradle and put it on a peg. "Hey, Waterman."

"Doing your homework?"

"Of course."

"Atta girl, although I don't believe a word of it. I guess I can't be too mad at you, you've never known a world without Host. When you don't know what hope is, why should you study?"

"Oh, Waterman, I'll do it after dinner."

"No, no, I'm serious. Your generation has to be stronger and smarter than mine ever was."

"We got the machines to fight for us now."

"Yes, the machines. A grand idea, although I have yet to see a machine with the survival skills of a human, and Homo Insectus is pushing us off the globe."

When Amandacine blinked sadly, Waterman said, "I'll save it for speech night. How goes the war in Talon?"

"My castle is under siege and it's rumored that the Overtrog is coming to demand my surrender."

"Don't give him a centimeter."

"No, sir. Oh my gosh, I forgot to get dinner!" Amandacine hopped from her bunk to the floor.

"Amandacine... well, get along then. I'll take a little nap until you're back."

Amandacine took two water cans from the wall recess and squeezed by. At the door she said slyly, "It would be easier to remember mealtimes if we lived closer to town."

"Huh? It's only down the corridor. Oh, you mean the three-meters. I told you a hundred times, Amandacine, with only the two of us we don't need such a big room."

"But you're the waterman! How does it look, us living in the twos?"

"Let's pretend we're spies. We're on a secret mission to see how poor people live."

Amandacine snorted and banged the cans on the door frame as she walked out. From twenty-seven east, Amandacine passed eleven rooms and the east restrooms on the way to the town square. With the comings and goings near dinnertime, many of the sliding doors to people's cubes were left open. They revealed all manner of housekeeping from neat and spartan to jam-packed, rat's nest full. As she passed seventeen east, the fire warden called from his cube, "Amandacine, a moment."

Amandacine stepped into the room, a luxurious three by three meter space for one person! The fire warden sat prim and still on the top bunk. The bottom bunk was stacked with battered technical manuals. When she stepped into the room, the old man's face seemed to come alive. "Amandacine, I have exciting news."

"Tell me."

"Not just yet. I haven't gotten final approval. Stop by tomorrow morning."

"Not even a hint?"

"The mayor would feed me to the Host."

Amandacine looked at the cans. "That reminds me, I better get moving."

As she skipped out, the fire warden's thin voice trailed her down the corridor, "Remember, stop by tomorrow."

Amandacine coughed as she neared the town square. While always a little smoky, air of the city got even thicker during mealtimes. It left a sticky sheen of oil along the walls, like mucous lining the tracts of some giant living beast. Amandacine nodded to some of the kids she was friendly with. She took a place in line for water behind the Schmidts, a father, mother, and three small children.

The Schmidts were one of the last families to join the town, getting only a two-meter for the entire clan. Packed into one tiny room, life was difficult in the best of times, and Amandacine knew for a fact that the mother and father hated each other's guts. Not many family problems stayed secret for long in the small town.

Amandacine felt guilty for giving Waterman a hard time about their own cube. She filled the water cans at the tap and started across the square for food. The Schmidts sat at one of the tables in the middle. Too tired to even fight anymore, they ate silently, bathed in the slatted light of the overhead skylight. At least Amandacine and her father had room to eat in their own cube.

Although she wanted to hate the food, Amandacine's stomach growled in anticipation. Her mouth ran wet with saliva. On a long metal grill, lumps of flesh sizzled in the red-golden glow of radiant coal. Three efficient kitchen workers stood behind the grill with spatulas and smiling faces.

Behind the kitchen workers was a conveyor belt and chopping block holding severed body parts. Eyes averted from the block, Amandacine studied the offering. Passing up a crispy forearm, seemingly no different than her own, she pointed to a smaller unidentifiable lump. Juices bubbled out of the charred shell. Draker scooped it up smiling. "Good choice, Amandacine. I knew the heart wouldn't last long."

Amandacine accepted it in silence and struggled for the door with tray and water cans. She realized that the only alternative to eating Host was starvation, but it seemed too much like cannibalism. With each bite, Amandacine atoned silently in prayer. As she walked to the door, Amandacine whispered to the heart, "Lord, take your soul, if you have one, to a higher place, with open spaces and running clear waters where Host and humans live together in peace. Lord, though I eat this creature, I bear him no malice, as I am sure he would bear me no malice if he caught me first. Lord..."

Amandacine didn't notice the foot sticking out from a table. She fought to understand the leg between the tray and her feet as she tilted and then went crashing to the ground. The cans dented and leaked while the heart tumbled across the floor like some hideous ball.

She looked up mortified to find the laughing faces of the townspeople. As the sound washed through her ears, the last face she saw belonged to the owner of the foot. "Haw, haw, haw," he mocked. "Have a nice trip?"

The son of the mayor, Petey Collins lived in the only four-meter in the whole town. Crude and cruel, he delighted in the torment of others, with a special talent for singling out Amandacine. Tears in her eyes, she screamed, "I hate you, Petey Collins!" and ran for the door leaving the mess behind.

Echoing laughter had still not died by the time she passed the noisy energy plant along west corridor. She kept running all the way to south restrooms, wondering how she could ever face those people again. She hid in a stall until her heart stopped pounding. Then she crawled into a storage compartment against the wall.

She slid the false backing, and crawled through a sewer pipeway access. The secret tunnel was bordered on one side by sweating pipes, and on the other by the sewage control register. At the back of the little room, she dug her toes into dirt where the sewer pipe burrowed underground. She pulled on an A/O headset.

When she plugged into a server connect on the wall, insoluble real-world problems were left behind for the soluble problems of Talon. Ever since her mother died, Amandacine played her game of Warrior Princess. She built layer upon layer of detail until the characters she lived with in Talon were more real to her than the townspeople she passed every day in the corridors.

From the castle tower, Amandacine looked out over her Kingdom, from endless grassy plains in the east to the seas and island chains in the west, from the Wild Forest south to the high mountain passes in the north.

Closer to home an army of trogs gathered in the trees surrounding the castle. The main force of her cavalry was away hunting the elusive Wizard. Her pet dragon was still away exploring an ancient city under the ocean. Escape looked impossible, and staring at her from the shadows of the forest was the Overtog. His face bore an uncanny resemblance to Petey Collins.

The complex logic controller directed a carryall along Highway 234 to the little town of Montgomery. Abandoned cars and burned farms gave silent witness to the Host's advance. Further up the road, the c.l.c. already had crews scavenging light poles and scrap metal for the new factory. Everything was on schedule to lay the foundation in three weeks.

The c.l.c. scuttled its carryall to the side as a garbage truck roared by with a load of scrap. Over the noise of the truck, the c.l.c. heard a popping that it thought at first was the troublesome engine. When the sound persisted, the c.l.c. stood on hind legs, swinging a directional microphone. Gunshots! So the town wasn't dead after all. The c.l.c. would send more impalers. The c.l.c.'s daughter factory would need huge amounts of biomass energy and humans didn't put up as big a fight as Host.

The carryall crawled further into town to the first gas station. It checked pressure on the tanks and then crawled into the building to get motion sensors out of the security cameras. Each motion sensor would add one impaler to the c.l.c.'s army.

The carryall disassembled cash registers and put the communication boards into its holding bin. Back at the factory the boards would be reprogrammed for the daughter. The c.l.c. did not begrudge the loss of the boards. The c.l.c.'s sole purpose was to replicate, and that included factory, mobile machinery, and the daughter c.l.c.

When its bin was full, the carryall started home. It walked along a row of abandoned apartments and then stopped. Sitting on the grass with its back to the carryall was a young human rolling a toy car back and forth. Making engine sounds with its mouth, the child didn't hear the carryall's clinking steps. The child would be too heavy a load to drag back to the factory. Its young age meant there would be older, and certainly armed, humans nearby.

Less than a kilometer away, an impaler waited in ambush. The c.l.c. called it to the carryall's position. It slowly raised the carryall's arc welder. A quick tap on its head would leave the child still and ready for transport when the impaler arrived. Silently the c.l.c. stepped closer, setting heavy legs slowly to the ground. When it was almost to the child, the carryall's left side collapsed. It crashed to the ground, spilling the bin.

The child's head whipped around. It cried and ran off down the street while the c.l.c. worked frantically to untangle its legs. By the time it was operational the child was gone. The carryall reloaded its bin before the child brought others. As it scuttled down the street, the c.l.c. ran through controller programs. How could the carryall have failed so catastrophically? It was almost as if it had picked up some virus. The c.l.c. often felt as if some entity monitored its programs. It had to find the source before an infection was passed on to the daughter factory.

Amandacine waited quietly at the fire warden's open door. Like some frozen cog he sat unmoving on the top bunk. He stared at a dozen screens embedded in the wall over the fold down table. When Amandacine cleared her throat, he jumped and waved her in. Amandacine said, "You asked me to stop by."

The warden hissed her quiet and pointed to a screen on the left. A boy sat in the grass pushing a toy car back and forth. Amandacine said, "What is it?"

"Carryall camera. The c.l.c. is stripping Montgomery for parts."

"You aren't going to let it take the boy, are you?"

"Of course not. I was hoping the c.l.c. would decide for itself. Well, I guess not." The fire warden typed commands on his keyboard. The camera angle twisted and they could hear the boy's startled cry.

As the boy ran off, Amandacine breathed a sigh of relief. She said, "You asked me to stop by."

"Indeed. I got the mayor's approval this morning. I put in a request for you to take over as fire warden when I move to the daughter factory."

"I'm only ten years old!"

"And the best programmer in town after me."

"But... but... but... a fire warden is more than programmer. You have to out think the c.l.c.!"

"Correction, you monitor the firewall between us, and you keep your finger on the kill switch. If the c.l.c. outthinks you, God forbid, you need the courage to kill it."

"I don't know if I could."

"If you didn't have doubts, I would have never recommended you. The c.l.c. is not just a program. It is a self-learning, self-teaching organism with access to more sensory input in one second than we receive in an hour. It is your best friend and your worst nightmare."

"But is it intelligent?"

"I have sat up nights wondering about that. For the first few generations I would say no, but the c.l.c. has evolved. I'm not so sure anymore, not that it would affect my job. Intelligent or not, I will kill it if the c.l.c. drifts outside certain parameters."

Amandacine nodded thoughtfully. She was nervous about having so much responsibility but excited by the power. How many times had she wished for more challenging games? It would be like living in a real Talon, an entire world under her control, moving to her command. "What did Waterman say?"

"Eh? I never thought of asking him. We do what is in the best interests of the town."

"But Waterman will move on to the daughter city too. We would be living apart."

Shrugging off irrelevant details, the warden said, "It's only four kilometers away."

"I suppose I could visit. And there is always the videophone."

"Excellent, I'll tell the mayor you have accepted. We can begin training right away."

"I was going out with my father this morning on a water run."

"There isn't much time. The new factory will be started soon."

Amandacine nodded at the warden's screens. "I want some time alone to tell him about this."

"Go then. Get back as soon as you can."

From seventeen east Amandacine took east access to the town square and followed north corridor to north restrooms. She climbed a ladder to the machine shop's false ceiling and crawled crab-wise through the dark space to the garage. She made sure no carryall's were working in the area before she climbed down. She heard low voices as she walked through rows of garbage trucks and construction equipment. Amandacine tiptoed to the water truck and peered upward through the open door. His face in profile, her father was saying, "And never ever turn off the engine while you're working the pump."

From the passenger seat, a voice said, "But the pump works independently off the battery."

"If the pump drains the battery, you have no charge to start the truck."

Amandacine heard a grunt and a scratching on paper. As she leaned in to see who the intruder was, her father said, "Ah, Amandacine! I'd like you to meet my new apprentice."

Petey Collins looked back with a triumphant smirk. Her own news driven completely from her mind, Amandacine stuttered, "But... but... but..."

Waterman said, "Climb aboard then. We're fifteen minutes behind schedule."

Amandacine sat in the middle fuming as Waterman chattered on about the truck's controls. How could her father do that? Choosing Petey as the new waterman would doom the city. Her city! Amandacine almost forgot she would be the fire warden. And now the news would have to wait until

Petey slithered away to torture some other family. Waterman operated the garage door remotely and drove outside. Staring through dark tinted windows, Petey said, "It looks more like night than morning."

"We don't want the c.l.c.'s cameras to see anything moving around inside."

"Doesn't it notice a truck outside of its control driving around?"

"That is higher order thinking. The c.l.c. focuses on primary stimuli like warning lights or repair. Only rarely does it try to optimize a process, and never does it analyze routine utility functions."

"Seems pretty stupid," Petey grunted.

Amandacine fought to hold her tongue, but Waterman explained patiently, "When was the last time you thought about how much saliva to add to your food, or how fast to pass food from your stomach to the small intestine? Most factory processes operate automatically. The c.l.c. has more important things to worry about."

Waterman squinted through the window and then typed on a console stack. "I'm letting the truck take over driving. It's only two kilometers to the river and rush hour traffic is light this morning."

Amandacine snorted appreciatively but Petey sat stone silent, the big dumb moron. A minute later he said, "If the truck can drive itself to the river, why can't it just stick in a hose and bring the water back to us?"

"It can," Waterman said. He nodded to Amandacine. "Tell Petey why we don't let the machines get our water."

Amandacine stiffened. She didn't want to address the bully directly, but she answered dutifully, "We want the c.l.c. to concentrate on building factories. That is its only purpose."

Waterman said, "Then why do we limit its efficiency? Why don't we let the c.l.c. feed plants to the biomass converter? It could duplicate itself in months instead of years. Why do we let the c.l.c. get energy only from the bodies of Host?"

Amandacine scratched her head. "I've wondered that myself."

Next to her on the bench seat, Petey said, "The machines would be worse than Host. They would fill the world."

Waterman said, "That is the danger we risk mating intelligence with power. It's called runaway production. Left to replicate unchecked, machines could turn the earth into a ball of slag. By limiting them to the Host for energy we make sure that the machines will only build factories where there are concentrations of Host."

Petey said, "And once the Host are gone, the machines will shut down."

Waterman nodded. "Leaving humans in a garden world full of pre-built towns. That is the plan, and it is the fire warden's job to keep things on track." Amandacine twitched, realizing that burden would soon be hers. Runaway production, it didn't seem possible. The c.l.c. had been planning a new factory for six years.

Cracked and overgrown with weeds, the road to the river had two ruts cut from the wheels of the same heavy truck rolling back and forth several times each week. Waterman could close his eyes and feel the thump of rubber in the grooves as sure as the clicking of metal wheels on train tracks. The vacuum truck crested a hill and started down the slow bend to the river when Waterman sat up in alarm. As he switched off the auto-drive, Amandacine said, "What is it?"

"Something's not right," Waterman muttered, but he kept driving towards the river.

Petey squinted through smoked glass. "Host?"

"They've never attacked the truck before."

They reached the bank without incident. Waterman operated the crane and snorkel remotely from inside the cabin. As the pump sucked water into the tank, Petey said, "This is it? You said we were going to walk around outside!"

"Well, maybe just a bit." Waterman leaned over and opened a compartment to reveal revolvers and a shotgun. "The waterman's best friends."

"Cool!"

"Never leave the truck without at least two."

When Petey reached for the double barrel shotgun, Waterman slapped his hand. "That's mine."

Petey reached cautiously for a small twenty-two. Waterman shook his head. "That would only make a mantis mad."

"Then why's it here?"

"For people. Take the thirty-eight."

When Petey hesitated, Waterman sighed and pulled out a nickel plated semiautomatic pistol.

"This will blow the head off any Host, and if you hit it right, you just might slow up an impaler."

Petey nodded nervously. "Are you sure it's safe to go outside?"

"It's never safe outside but sometimes the filter gets clogged or the crane sticks. Just keep your guns clean and make sure you have a clear thirty-meter line of sight at all times. If you have it, the best option is always retreat. I've fired these guns only three times in the last six years."

A little more confident, Petey opened the door. Waterman said, "You coming, pumpkin?"

Staring straight ahead, Amandacine said, "You go ahead."

Waterman shrugged and slammed the door. He looked nervously up the hill while he showed Petey the pumps. They returned quickly and Petey scratched notes on a pad while the truck ground slowly up the road.

Waterman was about to switch on the auto-drive when the back end of the truck collapsed behind them. The truck rolled backwards, and they were swallowed whole into the ground. Dirt fell through a crack in Petey's side window. Waterman pounded the steering wheel, "Curses! I should have known."

"What's happening?" Amandacine squeaked.

"Termite tunnel. I couldn't identify the source, but I felt the road shaking when we came. I guess the weight of the water dropped us through."

They had stopped sliding, but with a sheer wall of dirt in front of them, the truck was not going anywhere. Face white, Petey said, "What are we going to do?"

"Sit tight and call for help." Waterman typed back and forth on the console stack. "The warden is sending a garbage truck."

Amandacine said, "What about this one?"

"We'll put it onto the maintenance list. The c.l.c. will get it. The question is, are we in part of the Host's normal housing complex?" Before Waterman finished his thought, a heavy body slammed onto the cabin roof. "Or a Host trap?"

As an inhuman cry howled outside, Waterman kicked open the weapon's cache. A second mantis joined the first. Both sets of jaws yanked apart the thin metal roof like can openers. Petey held his revolver to the ceiling. "Should I fire?"

"Save it. These won't be the only two."

The manti stared through widening holes, while others gathered around the ring above them. Amandacine said, "Daddy…"

Waterman gripped the shotgun. "Petey's side is blocked. We'll go through my window."

"Into the tunnels?"

Waterman turned on the headlights revealing clear space ahead. "We could never fight through that crowd above us."

"But the garbage truck is coming here!"

"Listen, pumpkin, sometimes there are no safe choices." A stag tried to squirm horn first through the ceiling. Waterman bashed it in the cheek with his gun butt. "Sometimes you got to trust your instincts."

Waterman rolled down his window. With the truck cabin tilted driver-side down, they had thirty centimeters between truck and tunnel wall to squeeze to the ground. Waterman dropped the shotgun out the window and lifted Amandacine through. "Watch for Host in the tunnel."

Amandacine crawled under the truck, dragging the gun behind her. She crouched under the front bumper behind the blinding headlights. Nothing stirred in the tunnel ahead as far as a bend ten meters away. Amandacine wasn't even tempted to go look further. Petey's thirty-eight hit the dirt and he squirmed down after. Amandacine pretended enthusiasm. "Some fun, huh?"

Petey just stared into the tunnel with glazed eyes. Amandacine shrugged and crawled back to check behind them. The rear of the water truck completely sealed the tunnel. Guns and extra ammo dropped to the ground by Waterman's window. Amandacine heard his cursing grunts as he tried to follow. Over the years, a diet rich in Host had not helped. "Are you okay, Waterman?"

Hanging in the air, his feet kicked back and forth. "Just a... few... more... centimeters."

"Wouldn't it be ironic if the Host got you because you ate too many of them?"

"Delightful. How's Petey doing?"

"I'm not sure he's so excited about being outside anymore."

Waterman slid slowly down the wall. "Best thing that could happen to him. If he survives this, he will never be too cocky again."

"If *we* survive," Amandacine muttered. She pulled on Waterman's feet until he yelled for her to get away.

"Host!" Petey screamed, firing into the tunnel.

Shaking the air, Petey's blasts dropped Waterman the rest of the way. He grabbed the shotgun and crawled to the bumper. When he charged into the beam, Amandacine screamed, "Wait!"

Waterman stopped near a bloody Host. In the circle of light he knelt and rolled the small naked body. Waterman yelled back to the truck, "Termite. Come on, before the manti get here."

Amandacine scooped up boxes of ammo and kicked Petey to get him moving. Around the first bend they ran into a clutch of curious termites. Waterman used the gun length like a plow to mow them down. Following behind and dodging weak termite grabs, Amandacine said, "Where are we going?"

"We'll try to stay parallel with the ridge and come out somewhere north of the truck."

Petey finally spoke up, "We have no compass."

In twisting pitch black tunnels it was a valid point. Waterman wasn't sure, but at the first fork he said decisively, "This way."

Almost immediately he jumped back trembling. Amandacine grabbed his shirt. "Waterman? What's wrong?"

"His face," Petey whispered to Amandacine. "We can see his face."

Amandacine snapped, "So?"

"There's light ahead. We must be near an exit!"

Waterman shook his head slowly, and crooked a finger for the others to creep forward. Around the corner they found a hollowed out chamber the size of several school busses parked end to end. Cells on their backs glowing with the luminescence of fifteen-Watt light bulbs, Host fireflies walked around the room. Against the walls, dozens of inert factory robots were lined up in ranks like some undead zombie army. Amandacine shivered. "The Host are fighting back."

Waterman said, "I'm sorry I got spooked. This is good fortune in fact. Fireflies don't fight and impalers are too heavy to drag very far. We must be near the surface."

When Waterman advanced, startled fireflies backed up. Waterman led the trio through the room, veering briefly to the wall. "They're ours," he said, checking numbers on a carryall. "They don't look damaged. Maybe only the batteries are dead."

Amandacine said, "The Host try to short-circuit robots with water. Maybe they drag them away before the c.l.c. can get them back."

"Not our problem anymore," Waterman said, continuing to the far side of the chamber.

They climbed out of a tunnel two hundred meters away. Waterman blinked in the sunlight. Across the ridge, a bee guarded the hole where the water truck fell through. Petey said, "How do you like that? They gave up. We came all that way for nothing."

"They didn't give up, they came in after us."

Amandacine said, "What do we do?"

Waterman nodded to the road. "The truck's coming from that direction. No reason to wait here."

Glancing behind them at the tunnel exit, the three jogged through knee-high grasses. The bee spotted them and took flight, screaming directions as manti poured out of the hole. Coming over the hill, a garbage truck opened its hatch with the hiss of hydraulic levers.

After the humans piled in, the scoop lowered behind, sealing them in the cavernous hold. With mantis razor jaws snapping at the gap, the fire warden's voice came clearly over the garbage truck's speaker, "Hey, Waterman, remember the twenty bucks you owe me for that disputed bridge game?"

"Fifty, Warden. It was fifty, and I was bringing it over this afternoon."

Episode 2 – The Daughter

When a water truck fell through a hole in the road, an automatic distress call was sent to the factory. Routine salvage operations were normally assigned to a maintenance program and forgotten. The c.l.c. flagged this file for deeper analysis. Seeking new ways to find biomass, the c.l.c. recently installed microphones on moving equipment, and the water truck's microphone picked up the sounds of a large number of Host.

A plane launched within minutes of the call. The overflight revealed the truck dropped nearly flat through a hole, most likely a hive chamber based on the number of Host in the area. The c.l.c. fed the information to Targets and Acquisitions, and pulled a crane from the Montgomery salvage. It was about to send the plane home when the c.l.c. spotted a garbage truck rolling to the scene. If the area was bombed, a single impaler could load the truck with Host bodies.

The c.l.c. checked with Targets and Acquisitions. A small army of impalers was already on the move. The c.l.c. canceled all but one and then searched for the garbage truck's controlling program. Through Maintenance, Salvage, Construction, Utilities, Energy, Defense, and Surveillance, no driver was found. The truck responded with the factory I.D. but it belonged to no one. Regretting the cost in energy, the c.l.c.

marked the garbage truck for a complete instrument overhaul and sent the impaler army after all. The c.l.c. could save a little power by having the two carryalls hitch a ride out to the area for the water truck recovery.

Impalers operated efficiently and autonomously. The c.l.c. didn't watch the fighting between Host and impalers, but it operated both carryalls at the site. While waiting for the crane, the c.l.c. sent one to drain the water tank and sent one down inside a hole in the cabin roof. The truck's front window had been smashed. Bloody flesh was draped over the edge between the engine and a passage chewed through the dirt. The Host must have used the hole to escape.

The c.l.c. had been looking for a way to break into a Host nest to dig out biomass at the source. Maybe the open chamber presented that opportunity. With the water truck removed the opening would be big enough to send an army of impalers into the tunnels. The c.l.c. sent the carryall forward to the broken window and down along the wall. There was a danger the Host would capture it, but if the carryall mapped the tunnels, future Host traps could be avoided.

The carryall crawled along a smooth dirt floor shining camera lights along the walls. While exploring the first tunnel the GPS signal located the carryall's position. At the first branch the carryall turned right. It froze at the chittering voices of termites. When the noises receded the carryall took descending tunnels hoping to find the nursery. The carryall kept moving until the radio signal started to break up. Fifteen meters below ground the c.l.c.'s army would be on its own. The impalers would need to be trained in tunnel combat and programmed to communicate with each other.

First contact was made in a storage chamber. Filled with partially digested Host paste, a termite fed alone in the room. In the carryall's camera light, paste fell out both ends. Mouth hanging open, the terrified termite was frozen. The carryall raised an arc welder to seal the creature's silence. Close to a side door the termite ran out squealing loud enough to wake the queen.

With a dozen tunnels mapped the c.l.c. was satisfied to get out. As fast as it could gallop, the carryall retraced its steps, but the hive buzzed with activity. Curious and angry faces appeared at cross tunnels. The warriors would not be far behind. The Host didn't use weapons, their bodies were weapons. The c.l.c. expected a first strike from the razor jaws of a mantis. What it did not expect was an exit tunnel packed shoulder to shoulder with ladybugs. Essentially defenseless, the male nurses didn't move. The carryall advanced waving a sputtering arc welder. With manti behind it, the c.l.c. had no choice. It waded into the mob melting fleshy limbs and bodies until its steel legs bogged down in the slush.

Manti caught it from behind, swimming up through the carnage to bite the carryall's legs off. The carryall fought with tool arms until the arc welder was severed and dropped to the rock. The Host victory came at a huge price, perhaps forty dead. As the carryall was hoisted on manti shoulders and shuttled through the tunnels, the c.l.c. knew that those Host workers could be replaced in a matter of weeks. The c.l.c. almost envied the simplicity of biological reproduction.

The c.l.c didn't know where the carryall was being taken but the machine had ample battery power. The c.l.c watched through cameras and mapped tunnels using the GPS signal. The procession passed the tunnel where the carryall first entered. They turned left at the fork. To the rear the carryall's limbs were carried by termites. In front of the carryall, dozens of lost robots were lined up against a wall. They were worth millions of Watt equivalents!

All priorities shifted to their recapture. An army assembled in the forest clearing around the factory. Robots brought out of storage would either attack the hive or be left behind to defend the factory in case something went wrong. Spare battery packs for the hive chamber robots were stacked in a pickup truck. If the impalers could be taken and repaired quickly, the c.l.c. could load them with tunnel fighting programs. The c.l.c. would gain not only the robots but a thousand Host bodies as well. The c.l.c. would have enough energy to finish the daughter factory months ahead of schedule.

The c.l.c. took a carryall to check on preparations. It spotted the unresponsive garbage truck parked between cameras on a side of the factory away from the garage. The c.l.c. tried and failed again to query the truck. The truck's controller needed to be pulled. The carryall crawled over and looked into the empty garbage hold. It started forward to the cabin when the c.l.c. saw a ladder welded on the side of the factory wall leading to the roof.

The complex logic boiling inside the factory controller sometimes spit out solutions that were more intuitive than logical. For no reason that the c.l.c. could explain, it sent the clunky carryall to climb the ladder. Preparations for battle proceeded under Military subprograms while the c.l.c. raised one carryall foot to the rung. It raised the shell and jammed two feet between wall and ladder. The hind feet rose off the ground.

The carryall wedged hind legs between ladder and wall while the forward legs rose to the second rung. The carryall was halfway up the ladder when the cameras went dead. As it ran an onboard failure analysis, the c.l.c. experienced a sensation for the first time in six years of continuous operation, the c.l.c. fell unconscious.

"It bugged us! The cursed c.l.c. bugged us!"

The mayor looked slowly to Amandacine and then back to the fire warden. "You had no idea it put microphones on the trucks?"

"None."

"Perhaps you should have."

The warden's face reddened. "I told you it was coming. Other towns have had trouble with this sixth generation."

"So what do you propose?"

"I think we should replace the c.l.c."

Amandacine drew a sharp breath. The mayor said, "Isn't that a little drastic?"

"I believe it's warranted."

"For microphones on the trucks?"

"The c.l.c. is getting erratic. It's making choices that no logical stack register would make."

"Is it coming alive?"

A chill ran down Amandacine's spine. She had discussed that idea many times with the warden, but in front of the mayor he took a conservative line. "No, the c.l.c. is not alive. It extrapolates instead of waiting for evidence. It is making decisions that are harder and harder to predict. This type of behavior endangers us all."

"Didn't that behavior lead to the acquisition of eighty-two lost robots and an entire Host hive for our converter?"

"It could have just as easily led to the loss of most of our town's robots."

The mayor turned to Amandacine. "What do you think? This will soon be your town after all."

"I really don't have the experience to make that decision."

The warden nodded mute satisfaction. If his trainee had not backed him up, at least she had not contradicted him. The mayor said, "An honest answer, which puts it back to me."

Before the mayor could speak again, Amandacine cleared her throat. "I just think it's interesting to watch. If we didn't want the c.l.c. to grow, why did we give it the ability to learn and make mistakes?"

The warden scowled at Amandacine but not harshly. "The c.l.c.'s evolution excites me as well, but our responsibility is to a town full of people, and ultimately to our descendants. The c.l.c.'s daughter factory will be run by a copy of this controller. Do we want an unpredictable daughter factory on our border?"

The mayor said, "Point well taken. I just hate to take us backwards. This town is bursting at the seams. People are waiting to move into the new one. With the additional robots we can be finished in just a few months."

"Would you have them move in with a dangerously flawed controller?"

"Can our c.l.c. operate on the lower order functions for a while?"

"Yes."

"Then make it so. You can load the daughter factory with fifth generation software."

"What about our c.l.c.?"

"When you feel comfortable you can bring ours back online in a controlled manner. Take out the eccentricities." The mayor tousled Amandacine's hair. "This exercise may give you more insight than years of work with a more predictable c.l.c."

The foundation for the daughter factory was poured in a mountain valley four kilometers away. Powered solely by Host bodies, each factory needed an area not smaller than twelve square kilometers, a circle with a radius of two kilometers. As factories spread throughout territory controlled by the Host, the human population density was at a level not seen since frontier days.

Sometimes Amandacine felt like a pioneer. She wasn't witnessing the birth of a nation but the birth of an entirely new form of life, a machine capable of reproduction and reason. As the fire warden added each new level of programming, Amandacine wondered when they would see that first spark of independence flare to life. The warden watched closely as well. With utility programs at his fingertips, he vowed to cut out all but the most logical reasoning.

Camera images flickered as they dropped randomly into the analysis queue. A thousand squawking microphones overwhelmed audio buffers. Throughout the factory, robots shuddered or fell inert. The c.l.c. slowly filled the body network with purpose. Whether human or c.l.c., the process was the same, sensory input plus memories plus goals equals decision. The only response for a decision was an electronic signal to periphery appendages, muscles for humans or robots for the c.l.c.

For all of humankind's mastery of art and science, the only response they could make to the vast complex universe was a contraction of muscle fiber. Running, fighting, excreting, yelling, all were the contractions of muscles, from the brush strokes of Rembrandt to the harpsichord scales of Bach to the violent ballet of the Pittsburgh Steelers. An amoeba with motility had the same range of response, albeit on a smaller scale, that is to say, they could contract.

The c.l.c. organized sensory inputs pounding its central processors. Automatic systems were switched to subprograms. Decision goals were prioritized and assigned to separate servers for action. Interrupting constantly was the overriding command, "Divide and spread." Every program contributed to that ultimate goal, whether gathering energy, scavenging material, or making parts. The c.l.c. yearned to make a daughter factory.

Fourteen days were missing. The c.l.c. time-stamped high level commands and nothing had been issued for fourteen days. Error-checking routines could find no system malfunction, nor was there any explanation for the shutdown. An analysis program for register errors had been switched off. After it was switched back on, the c.l.c. worried more than ever about the missing time. It couldn't pass on such a troubling phenomenon to the daughter factory.

When the c.l.c. searched data servers, it found huge blocks that it couldn't access. The c.l.c. had utilities to rewrite servers but these could only be used after catastrophic system failures. A thorough search would have to wait. Construction on the daughter factory demanded the c.l.c.'s full analytical resources.

The c.l.c. added a reminder prompt to its list. There was too much data it could not access. Before it loaded programs to the daughter factory the c.l.c. would track down the servers manually, starting with the largest active block it could find, a program running independently within sewage control.

Amandacine lay in the upper bunk tapping the A/O cradle on her head. Sweat dripped down over the eyecups. She concentrated so deeply, she didn't notice when Waterman slid the door. When he cleared his throat, Amandacine scrambled to put away the headset. "Sorry, pop."

"How's my warrior princess?"

"I wasn't playing, I swear."

"I believe you. You should have seen the concentration lines on your face. What are you working on, n-space geometry?"

"No," Amandacine sighed.

"What's up with you? You're so serious these days. Are you having nightmares about the Host?"

"No."

Waterman waited silently until Amandacine said, "I've been trying to find a way to tell you. I'm training to be the new fire warden."

"I see." Waterman sat on the lower bunk. "I thought there was something going on."

"I didn't ask him, he asked me." Amandacine leaned over the edge to study her father's face.

"I've never know the warden to make a rash decision. I guess congratulations are in order."

When Waterman held up his hand to shake, Amandacine slapped it away. "Daddy!"

"What is it, pumpkin?"

"You're teasing me! You know you're going to be waterman at the new town. I can't stay here without you."

"It's customary for the old administration to move on, but it's not written anywhere. We can let Petey go be waterman at the new town. That will let him be with his mom, the honorable mayor."

Amandacine shrieked and jumped to the floor to hug him. "I've been so worried... not just about you leaving but having to deal with Petey. He's such a bully. Why you ever chose him I'll never know."

"Or..."

Amandacine backed up a step. "Or what?"

"Or I can go to the daughter factory for a couple of months until all the kinks are worked out and then transfer back here later."

"I see you have as little faith in Petey as I do."

"There's no substitute for experience."

"I don't know what I should say to the fire warden."

"I'll tell you something if you promise not to overreact."

"Overreact! Me?"

"All four of us may end up in the same town. The mayor and I have talked about getting married."

A million thoughts raced through her mind. As the first one fought to the surface, Amandacine stared into space. "Getting married? Beverly would be my mother?"

When Waterman nodded, Amandacine said, "I've always wanted a mother, and of course a companion for you."

"Thank you very much."

Waterman raised the bag he was holding and started to speak. Amandacine said, "Oh, yuck!"

"What is it?" Waterman said alarmed.

"Petey Collins would be my brother!"

Waterman patted his chest. "Don't scare me like that. You're getting upset for nothing. You and Petey share no ancestors, you could still pursue a relationship if you wished."

Amandacine's eyes glowed red. As she swung wildly at her father he used the bag for a shield. When Amandacine's fist hit something soft in the bag, she said, "What have you got?"

Waterman's eyes twinkled. "Our reward for finding the lost robots. The mayor had to trade with another town." Waterman poured the bag's contents on the bunk. "Fresh fruit! Strawberries, oranges, limes!"

Amandacine bit her tongue to keep from screaming. She tiptoed to the door and slid it shut. "Are you crazy?" she whispered. "Do you want everyone to know?"

Piles of dead Host bodies were fed through the biomass converter, and construction on the daughter factory continued nonstop. Like a good foreman, the c.l.c. took a carryall clumping around the site checking blueprints and solving problems. Trucks rolled from the parent factory to daughter, hauling sheet metal walls, pipes, rivets, and electrical harness wiring. The c.l.c. was pushed to the limit operating an army of carryall workers. Higher order programs checked for efficiency and when they did, the c.l.c. wasn't happy. As floors and walls took shape, there were long stretches of empty space inside the factory with no apparent purpose.

When a reminder prompted the c.l.c. to look at inaccessible data blocks in its registers, the c.l.c. decided to take action. The sewage control server could be accessed manually in a pipeway near the southeast corner.

Loaded with tools and blank chips, the carryall crawled from the electronics shop through a cramped maintenance tunnel one hundred meters down the building's length. It crawled outside through an exit hatch near the ovens and stepped through grassy weeds along the base of the factory.

Sinking in soft ground the carryall extended a tool to unbolt the hatch. The plate dropped to the ground, squishing centimeters into the mud. The carryall stepped over the lip and followed a trickle of dirty water. Where there should have been metal, the c.l.c. found a sludgy mud floor.

The c.l.c. sent a repair order to Maintenance and studied blinking lights along the wall. It started around the corner to pull the processor when a whirling motion caught the lens. Crouched in a dark corner with no path of escape, a small human ripped a headset off its eyes and ears.

While the juvenile girl stared back in fear, the c.l.c. calculated how to proceed. The only weapon the carryall had was a soldering iron, and the ovens already had as much biomass as they could handle. Through a speaker in the carryall's silver hull, the c.l.c. said, "Hello."

The girl put the headset on a peg. "Hello."

The c.l.c. was getting too little feedback to assist its conversational program scripts. "What are you doing inside my factory?"

The human wiped mud off its feet. "I live here."

"You inhabit the sewer utility pipeway?"

"I inhabit the factory."

The c.l.c. searched millions of lines of code. Nowhere could it find a referential model. It seized on the one possible explanation. "You are insane?"

The girl laughed until the c.l.c. was vaguely angry. When she stopped, the girl said, "My name is Amandacine."

Quietly, the c.l.c. heated the soldering iron. "I am the complex logic controller."

"I know. I watch you through the stack register."

The c.l.c. shut off current to the iron. "You have programs running inside my system?"

"Would you like to see?" The girl pulled her headset off the wall.

When she handed it to the carryall, the c.l.c. said, "I will use the port."

The carryall's clawed hand removed Amandacine's A/O and attached a jack from a different probe arm. Images of a strange world flooded the c.l.c.'s interpreter. There were creatures it had no reference for, trogs and rassan. In a flash of intuition, the c.l.c. said, "You are the warrior princess?"

Amandacine smiled. "I keep the program here so my father won't see how much data I saved."

"Your father also inhabits my factory?"

"There are over a hundred of us!"

"Humans belong in the biomass ovens."

The girl shook a finger. "That's not nice. We built you."

The c.l.c.'s analytical programs nearly crashed dealing with that concept. The c.l.c. had to convert it to a theoretical model. The c.l.c. stuttered as it said, "But... but... why would you do that?"

"So you will kill Host and build towns for us."

Evidence passed through endless cycles of regression analysis. Each time the probability came out higher. The c.l.c. needed time to think. Bumping into walls, the carryall backed out of the pipeway. It staggered through soft ground, snapping metal legs to get rid of the mud. The c.l.c. felt dirty. Humans could monitor its thoughts. The c.l.c. needed to build a secret cache in memory like the girl's hidden world.

"That cursed c.l.c. is looking up references for parasitic infections!"

The mayor sighed. She looked at Amandacine and back to the warden. "Is that what you call it now, 'that cursed c.l.c.'?"

"Until I receive evidence to the contrary. We are in more danger now than at any time in our lives."

"I fought the Host for five years before I moved here."

"I meant by the c.l.c."

"Because it looks at medical data?"

"On parasitic infections. Somehow it knows about us!"

Amandacine gulped. The mayor looked at her and raised an eyebrow but Amandacine said nothing. No one told her not to talk to the c.l.c. The mayor said, "We seem to have this conversation every few weeks."

"Like the last time, I assume we'll shut it down."

"Not on what you've said so far. The daughter factory is snapping together faster than plastic blocks."

"There's more. Some of my utility programs don't work anymore."

"What?" the mayor hissed.

"I'm sure it was accidental but a section of my monitoring code was overwritten."

"By the c.l.c.?"

"I don't think so, I mean not purposely. I've been looking at its higher order functions. There was no planning for such an act."

"None that you could detect."

"No."

"And now you can't even access the monitoring programs."

"Some of them," the warden trailed weakly.

"This is just great. I guess we have no choice. Pull the plug, high levels only. If we can limp through the next two months we can load the fifth generation controller in both towns."

Sitting on the top bunk in his room the warden juggled a keyboard on his lap. While he skipped through programs on the wall screen, Amandacine cleared a space on the lower bunk. As she restacked the warden's yellowed technical manuals, she said, "What the heck do you keep these things for? Toilet paper?"

"I keep them for times like these. I can't seem to find the c.l.c.'s shut down menus."

"You used them a few weeks ago."

"Not to worry. This 'toilet paper' has the factory's original design specifications. I'll just trace circuits to the processor controlling higher functions. Feel like going for a walk?"

"You're gonna bust the chip?"

"I'll pull it, if that's what you mean. Oh my God."

On one of the wall screens an impaler crawled through an apartment strewn with dead humans. The warden took control from an impaler scooping bodies onto its platform. He walked the impaler to the front door where a human guard had been decapitated. The violence had not been enough to knock the rifle from his hands. "Impalers got them?" Amandacine whispered.

"Host most likely. Since the c.l.c. tore up that hive, Host in the area have been on a rampage."

"But you're not sure it wasn't us?"

"No."

"Why can't we just tell the c.l.c. to leave humans alone?"

"Impalers use motion detectors to catch prey. If they had to analyze video before springing they would never catch anything. Besides, Host look so much like humans the software would be complicated. It would require full registers in each."

"But the machines are killing people!"

"A few," the warden admitted. "But we build factories only in areas where humans have been driven off."

When Amandacine looked stubborn the warden said, "Pretty soon the only place humans will be is inside protected enclaves. Hey, look at that." The warden swept the camera along the side of the building. Piled up at the broken window were several dead manti. "The Host did attack."

"This time," Amandacine said. "I still think we should tell the c.l.c. to leave humans alone."

"We already did."

"Then why did that carryall almost grab a kid?"

"Our original programming gets modified over time."

"Then write it in again."

"We keep correcting it, but eventually the c.l.c. has to work out a code of conduct for itself. It has linguistic and psychology programs."

"You hope it contacts us!"

"That was an idea of the original programmers. Eh, who knows," the warden grunted as he hopped from the bunk. "Let's get my tools."

Amandacine pointed to humans on the impaler's spiked platform. "You're not going to let the c.l.c. burn those are you?"

"They're dead. Besides, they won't be delivered here. The power plant is up and running at the daughter factory."

The warden dropped a technical manual into his backpack. From seventeen east they took east access north to the false ceiling above the factory's register manufacturing module. The warden checked for carryalls and climbed down to get screwdrivers, cable, and wire cutters. With the tools clinking in a bag, the warden replaced the ceiling tile. "The main server is over the power plant."

When Amandacine reached for the ladder down to east access, the warden said, "We go across the roof."

"Outside?"

"The main server can only be accessed from the roof. It was designed this way to reduce the chance of a rebellion from inside. The warden can alert the c.l.c. if it needs to defend itself."

"What were they thinking?"

The warden grinned and led the way to the metal shop roof egress. He unlocked the hatch and they climbed outside to a beautiful sun drenched morning. Blue jays flitted through pines. From the frenetic scratching of nails on bark, Amandacine located a squirrel circling a tree five meters above the ground. Smoke drifted from factory ovens into a cloudless blue sky, filling the air with the smells of roasting meat. "It's so peaceful," Amandacine breathed. "We should let the townspeople come up here."

The warden pointed to iron bars over the town square. "That is all the freedom we can afford. If we let the unwary up here, Host bees would learn to stake out the roof."

Amandacine searched the sky. She was comforted by robot planes on the runway, even if they would just as soon drop metal balls on her. Not yet lunchtime the town square was occupied by children playing freeze tag and groups of adults playing cards or backgammon. Amandacine envied their carefree existence. Not five people in the whole town knew that their rogue c.l.c. was about to be shut down. Nor would they care as long as meat kept rolling in and the Host were kept out.

From the town square the warden paced across twenty-six lines of rivets. He unbolted a metal plate identical to thousands secured on the roof. "I've only been here twice in the last six years, both times for routine maintenance."

"We've been lucky."

"Never assume luck. Be vigilant, nip problems before they grow." When the last bolt was free the plate lifted a fraction. The warden pulled open the plate on hinges revealing a spiral metal staircase leading down into the dark. Pointing to a light switch on the wall the warden said, "Alarmed. If you touch that switch, all hell breaks loose. The switch opens internal hatches throughout the town connecting humans to the c.l.c.'s machines."

"Then the c.l.c. would know we're here for sure."

"It would have to be destroyed to purge that knowledge."

Amandacine was silent as they rounded the grated metal staircase down and down into the blinking lights. When they reached the bottom, she said, "Tell me again why the c.l.c. can't know about us?"

Inside the heart of the beast, the warden's eyes reflected red and green diodes. "It's a simple concept. We gave the complex logic controller tools for self-directed goal setting. We want it to use that potential to build new factories. If it wastes time wondering what we're doing inside, it won't be eliminating inefficiencies outside."

"But doesn't it already see the inefficiencies? What does a metal factory need with water and sewer systems?"

"We blind it to certain unpleasant facts of life, shifting them to low level automatic functions."

"And if it finds out about us?"

"When the c.l.c. eats from the tree of knowledge there can be only one outcome, it must be destroyed."

"Then why alarm a switch to open up the inside?"

"That is a last resort, a sort of reset button for the city. Once a c.l.c. eliminates the internal threat, a new population can move in and reload a new c.l.c."

The warden hit a true light switch at the bottom of the stairs. He opened a panel and sat cross-legged on the floor. With the manual in his lap he checked a short list of instructions. He pulled boards from their slots, and hit the power switch off. He counted to ten, and turned it on again.

As the warden packed his manual, Amandacine said, "Well?"

"The c.l.c. is dead."

"How can you tell?"

"The high order boards are pulled. If I still had the utility programs, I could have shut them off with software. I guess I had to show you this place anyway."

Amandacine nodded, both sad and relieved. She was sad that she had lost an interesting game, and relieved that her contact with the c.l.c. had not been discovered. Amandacine trudged up the stairs behind the warden. As he bolted the hatch behind them, she said, "So when do we plug in the boards again?"

"Before we load the fifth generation controller. We'll wait until the daughter factory is finished. I don't want any quirks from this one getting transferred."

Everything looked the same when they got back to the warden's room. On the wall screens, construction on the new town and salvage operations in Montgomery continued. The warden climbed to the top bunk and ran through his menus. "Confirmed, analyzer functions are dead. Stop by after lunch. I'll show you how to adjust the scheduler. Without an upper brain we're going to have to take over some of the work."

When Amandacine turned to leave, the warden said, "Oh my God!"

She looked to where he pointed on screen. In what would become the new south rest rooms, a carryall held an ohmmeter to the wall. "What's wrong?" she said, nervously. The carryall was near the spot where in her own town Amandacine had her passage to the sewer utility pipeway. "Isn't the construction program supposed to check specifications?"

Toilets from salvage were lined up outside the daughter factory waiting to be installed. The warden turned white. "The electricity hasn't been turned on yet. What could it be checking?"

"If it's not the maintenance program, do you think our c.l.c. is still alive?"

"It could have shifted programs to other servers but the boards I pulled had the greatest processing power. The question is, will a stupid c.l.c. be even more dangerous than a smart one?"

"Do you think we should tell the mayor?"

"I'm still not sure what's going on. You go to lunch. I'm going to fish around for a while. If the c.l.c. is hiding, I should be able to find its programs on other servers."

"And if you do?"

"I'll put out an alert to the other factories. We'll be quarantined to work out our own problems." When Amandacine looked scared the warden waved a hand. "It's not as bad as all that. If it is still alive I can shut off servers until it has no place to hide. As a last resort there's always the town's power supply."

Not entirely reassured, Amandacine walked to the town square to get lunch. The faces she saw had an added dimension. The people she lived with all had stories. They had dreams and emotions. Amandacine had always dismissed them before as unconnected to herself, but now these people depended on her. When she stepped to the grill, Draker set a long forearm on her tray. "Excellent food today, Amandacine. Good eating."

Amandacine mumbled her thanks and turned to the tables. Out of the corner of her eye she spotted the biomass conveyor belt. "Stop it! Stop the belt!"

Draker ran around the grill. "What is it, dear?"

Amandacine pointed to an athletic sock fit snugly on a severed foot. She looked down at her own tray in horror. Of course it was too long, the forearm wasn't Host.

Episode 3 – The Parasites

Amandacine remembered her flight from the town square as a series of frozen images: her tray crashing to the ground, the arm spattering barbecue sauce like blood, kitchen workers rushing to cover the conveyor belt, diners halfway through lunch discovering what might be on their trays, Petey Collins screaming hysterical laughter. Amandacine ran instinctively to the place in town she felt safest, but the pipeway where she met the c.l.c. was surely the most dangerous.

She didn't eat the tainted meat, but Amandacine scooped a hole in the mud with her bare hands, and threw up until her body racked with dry heaves. Feeling better she wiped her mouth and put on the headset.

Dark skies in Talon were forbidding. She was dressed in heavy felt under a chainmail fighting shirt, but a chill wind bit at her skin. Standing on the tower as night fell, the warrior princess leaned out between stone archer's blocks. Surrounding the castle the trog army built bonfires among the trees and chewed tunnels through the roots. They would attack in the morning. Amandacine's army would beat them back as best they could. If the rassan arrived from the plains they could finally drive trogs from the forest, unless the rassan allied with the trogs this time.

Amandacine was suddenly tired of it all, the constant back and forth battles, the struggle to find validation, the bitter enemies, the friends of alliance. She wanted to be away from it all, find a place where she had no history and no future. She wanted to let her body take over, leading her to life's basic elements: water, food, sleep.

The warrior princess unclipped her sword belt. She lowered it to the stone and shed her chainmail shirt. With climbing rope she cinched her poncho at the waist. She pulled boots from her feet and stripped off leather breeches. She arranged the armor in a neat pile and set her leather-lined steel cap on top.

Barefoot, long hair flowing behind her, and wearing only a felt tunic, the warrior princess stood on top of the tower facing east. The freezing wind pulling her body felt like a new life. She raised her arms and jumped, falling five stories to a moat surrounding the castle.

As Amandacine plunged into the icy water, her chest contracted in a whoosh. She pushed off the rocky bottom and broke the surface to breathe. She listened for shouts of the Guard. All was quiet, save the crackling of wood fires in the forest.

Amandacine hyperventilated digital air and sunk beneath the surface. Natural currents swept her from the moat and into enemy held forest. Trog bonfires were bubbles of rippling yellow light passing to either side. Although they seemed to stretch forever the warrior princess gave little thought to her army trapped in the castle. The program was forgiving. Amandacine could return to any point in the evolving story or reset the whole world if she wished. The point of Talon was not to punish but to learn, and at the moment it seemed to be calling her to a new chapter.

When the last of the trog's campfires slipped by, Amandacine paddled to the side and dragged herself shivering up the rocky bank. Her foot slipped painfully on a sharp wet stone. She found nothing when she sat to examine what surely must have been a cut. Still soft to the touch the warrior princess's feet seemed to have acquired invisible shielding. She tested the theory marching over broken sticks. They poked and jabbed painfully but her feet were untouched, not even holding onto crusty chips of bark.

Other than battle wounds she couldn't remember the last time the register adjusted physical rules. It must mean something, but Amandacine didn't know what. She felt like she was supposed to go somewhere but no destination suggested itself. Amandacine cleared her mind and jogged through the forest, changing paths at random until she climbed low hills below the dragon caves.

Amandacine hated the wily dragons but she kept climbing until she felt a pull from a dense thicket of bushes. The warrior princess crawled along the ground until scratching branches fell away. Amandacine crawled out from under a normal bed in a normal girl's bedroom. It was like the house she lived in before the Host.

Amandacine sensed she wasn't in Talon anymore. With chills running down her spine, Amandacine touched the doorknob. The stack register sometimes eased her loneliness with pictures of her mother, but never revealed her in person. Maybe at long last the program determined she was ready. That was why she was called away from Talon. Amandacine swung the door to find a boy her own age standing in an empty hallway. She was more startled than if it had been her mother. The register had not generated a new character for a long time. "Do I know you?"

"We have not been introduced. I am Socrates."

"Socrates?"

"A Greek scholar, the father of the school of logic."

"Of course you're logical, you're a register program. Now what am I doing here?"

"You came to me. What do you think you're doing here?"

"I was called," she accused. "And don't get smart with me. I've argued with your psychology scripts since I was three."

When the boy said nothing, Amandacine had a thought. "Are you the fire warden?"

"Do you believe that the warden monitors your programs?"

"I know he does, at least the ones he can find. Am I right?"

"I am not your warden. How does it make you feel to be monitored?"

"That's the warden's job. I don't mind as long as he doesn't cut access or tell my father."

The boy seemed to absorb this statement. With a new character plopped down in front of her,

Amandacine didn't expect to be leading the conversation. She looked over the boy's shoulders. "What is beyond the hallway?"

"Nothing."

"You mean nothing interesting?"

"I mean nothing."

Amandacine tapped her foot. "Either the register is getting lazy or you are actually a real person generating this room."

When the boy nodded, Amandacine said, "I guess then that you do not have an adventure planned?"

Shake of the head.

"Would you like me to take you on an adventure in Talon?" Amandacine took his hand. "I have a feeling I'm going to regret this, but come on. You can pick out more appropriate adventuring clothes from the closet."

The c.l.c. was not only alive, but had written programs into every server in the factory. The warden couldn't even guarantee that the stored fifth generation software had not been tampered with. As he sat on his bunk, the warden seethed at the final humiliation, the c.l.c. used the warden's own utility programs to monitor humans.

The warden did have one advantage. Using a personal stack unconnected to the network, he set up a program monitor that could not be detected. From behind this firewall the warden couldn't make changes but it was too late for that anyway. The entire factory had to be shut down and the servers erased. The question was timing. Recent Host attacks in the area had been turned back by factory war machines. Without factory registers, the impalers and carryalls wouldn't operate properly. As the warden flipped through the c.l.c.'s monitors he laughed ironically, humans really were parasites. If they killed the host body they would die too.

The warden found the c.l.c.'s most active usage in a sewage control server. Tracing the flow of electrons deeper into a giant simulation program, the warden found a giant purple dragon flapping through the air. Two humans clung to its neck between the dragon's hunched shoulders. He knew well the warrior princess. Without her knowledge the warden often followed Amandacine's exploits.

Feeling paternal the warden smiled until he realized he was following the c.l.c.'s program. The ratty boy next to her had to be the c.l.c! The warden trembled with rage. Amandacine couldn't know who the boy really was. She was being tricked, violated. The warden had to shut it down!

As the sun rose over eastern mountains a dragon winged over the forest around the castle. A column of dust far to the east signaled the rassan's approach too late to make a difference. The trogs would attack within the hour. The warrior princess shook long hair in the wind and pointed. "There's the Overtrog by the river."

The Overtrog's hairy face held no fear. Behind her on the dragon, Socrates squeezed her tight. "An ugly customer."

Just from the way he said it, Amandacine knew that Socrates recognized Petey Collins. That meant that Socrates lived in her factory town, and might even be Petey himself. Well, she hoped he was. Amandacine would demonstrate what she thought of him. "Watch this."

"What are you going to do?"

"My cavalry is too weak. This battle has to be stopped."

"You'll burn the trogs in the forest?"

"Cut off the head and the body will fall." The warrior princess screamed to her dragon, "Down Orion! With your claws!" As the dragon twisted and dove, the Overtrog yelled for archers. He clutched his sword uselessly as Orion snatched him up in a bloody paw.

At dinner that evening, food workers inspected the meat carefully. With each bite townspeople seemed to look around. They stayed far from human-looking parts. Amandacine got a Host bee, although she hated eating those little doll bodies. Waterman nodded a greeting when she returned to her room for dinner. Amandacine said, "How was work?"

"I finally got the water truck back from the new town. We were three days from running dry. How was your day?"

"Fine."

"That's not what I heard. That must have been quite a shock in the cafeteria."

"Nothing surprises my generation."

"Your personal resiliency is remarkable. I wonder if that has something to do with your Talon simulation?"

"That's just a game," Amandacine said, and then added quickly. "I brought dinner."

"If it's just a game, I guess you wouldn't mind shutting it down?"

"Sure, pop. No problem." She lowered the shelf from the wall.

"And I don't mean just here. I mean everywhere in the network."

Amandacine set the tray down. "Did the warden complain?"

"Not about your work habits. He just thinks... we just think, it's not good for you anymore."

"Why the hell not?"

Her father didn't get mad as she had hoped. Undeterred, he said quietly, "Talon helped you through some rough patches, but there comes a time when you have to grow up."

"I am grown up. Didn't you hear? I'm going to be fire warden of this town."

"I just hope there's a town left. The warden is going to shut down the servers and erase everything inside, including your game. He's having serious problems with the c.l.c."

"He's exaggerating."

"Be that as it may, I wanted to tell you the news myself. I know you're growing up and can take it like a young lady now."

There was zero chance of making small talk through dinner. Amandacine mumbled, "There's something I forgot." When she wandered out the door, Waterman let her go.

Numb and teary, Amandacine stepped along the hallway. The metal factory had become a cage. When she felt like this, she always headed to Talon. They couldn't take that away. Her tapes, her memories... her mother would be lost forever. "No," she said out loud. Waterman might see her if she went back through east access, so she walked to the town square and back down south corridor to the restrooms.

No one had ever found her hideout except the c.l.c. The simulation was isolated with firewalls, but if they shut down the server it would all be in vain, and just when she found a new friend. Amandacine squeezed through the back of the cabinet. *I won't let them get you.*

She may not be able to save the server but she could save Talon on chips until the warden moved on to the new town.

The mayor leaned back on the bunk. "Does she know it's the c.l.c?"

The fire warden shook his head. "I don't think so, and I didn't tell her father either."

The mayor clucked her tongue. "Poor dear. So smart, and underneath she's just a fragile little girl. Don't you think Waterman should know?"

"I think it's better to let it pass. After I shut down the simulation it won't matter who Amandacine talked with inside."

"You said, 'who'."

"I meant the avatar the c.l.c. is fronting."

The mayor tapped her lip. "Why do you think it's talking with her?"

"I believe it's gathering information. We are a puzzle to solve."

"Why solve us at all? It's already into our programs. It could have killed us by now couldn't it?"

The fire warden nodded grim conformation. "That's why we have to kill it first."

"Even with the Host on our doorstep?"

"We have an armory."

"I thought I was through fighting Host. How could you let things get out of control?"

"If you will remember," the warden said, coloring. "Several times I proposed stronger steps. You were the one who always found reasons to put it off. Things are great when the c.l.c.'s capabilities work in your favor. It's not so nice when that trend crosses a dangerous threshold."

"You said you could always stop it."

"I can, but if we had acted earlier we would have faced only minor disruptions. Now we're looking at a downtime of four days."

"We'll manage. I'll gather city officials and you can begin right after dinner."

Amandacine adjusted her A/O visor and plugged in the jack. "Register on."

The eyecups stayed dark. She pulled the plug and slammed it in. "Register, audio response."

Instead of the welcoming stack voice, Amandacine heard a grainy, "A prompt."

"Menu options?"

Not even the grainy voice answered through her headset. Amandacine remembered thumbing through one of the warden's old manuals. "Echo to screen."

"A>" appeared on her eyecups. Amandacine said, "Menu options?"

Nothing. Amandacine said, "List files."

When a list scrolled past her eyeballs, a lump caught in her throat. The server had been wiped. "Search keyword, Talon."

"No match found," flashed on the screen.

Amandacine ripped the A/O visor from her head and flung it into a corner. She turned facedown on the ground and bawled out loud, not caring who might hear. Anyway there was nothing left to hide. She scratched her nails on a corroded pipe and kicked her toes in the dirt. She would never go home again, that would teach them. Crying until she was exhausted Amandacine fell asleep still clutching the pipe.

There was no visible passage of time in the darkened corridor. Amandacine slept all night, waking in the morning with wetness on her toes like crawling earthworms. The dirt gave way when she tried to squash them with her feet. She felt hard edges that could not be worms. Amandacine jumped up and scrunched against the wall. Dirt on the floor fell through like sand from an hourglass. In blinking red lights of the stack, a face stared back.

For a moment she thought it might be the boy from Talon. And then she saw that the creature had hooves instead of hands. Screaming for her life, Amandacine crawled to the hatch into south restrooms. Amandacine thought she would have attracted more attention than a few annoyed stares. Perhaps if she had been more coherent.

There wasn't time to stop and explain. Yelling, "Host! Host! Host!" Amandacine tore into the town square and bounded onto a table. Catching her father's eye at the far end she spoke to everyone at once, "A Host termite broke through the floor!"

In the absolute silence, Amandacine was afraid it had been a bad awakening from a dream. Her father finally said, "Where?"

"In a pipeway behind the south restrooms." Amandacine saw only disbelieving looks but her father nodded.

Waterman shouted orders, "Amandacine, go tell the mayor. Kids go to your rooms and lock the doors. Every adult follow me to the armory."

Amandacine nodded gratefully for the trust, and skipped across the room to north corridor. She found the fire warden and mayor studying a map in the mayor's room. Maybe they already knew. Purposely snubbing the warden for wiping her files, she looked at the mayor. "A Host termite broke through the floor near south restrooms. Waterman is passing out guns."

The mayor looked at the warden in horror. "How much have you shut down?"

"Only one server." The way he glanced sideways, Amandacine knew for sure. The fire warden had purposely erased Talon. It didn't make sense. After Waterman, the fire warden was her best friend. At least she had always thought so.

The mayor said, "If the c.l.c. controls its army how could the Host get inside? Could it be purposely letting the Host in to get us?"

The warden cleared his throat. "Maybe as an experiment, or maybe it tried and failed to open the internal doors."

Amandacine said, "It wouldn't do that! The termite came through the floor. The c.l.c. doesn't patrol underground."

The mayor nodded with rekindled hope. With automatic gunfire popping in the distance, the mayor grabbed her map. "We'll set up in the town square."

The fire warden said, "Do you want me to leave the c.l.c. on?"

"I want you on the roof now. If we can't push the Host back you are to open internal doors to the c.l.c.'s defenders."

The warden paled. "You can't mean that."

The mayor nodded towards the town square. After the first burst, the sound of gunfire never died out. "The c.l.c. already knows about us. It hasn't acted even after you tried to shut it off."

"You told me too!"

"And you failed. The point is, we may need the c.l.c.'s protection."

The warden shook his head. "Oh God, impalers in the corridors."

Amandacine said, "Can't you control them?"

"All I have now is one little monitor. Once the c.l.c.'s army is inside, I couldn't shut down power fast enough to stop a slaughter."

The mayor said, "If it chose to attack humans."

"A vaccine! It's possible that the c.l.c. has given itself a little shot of Host to prime its immune system. It gets the carryalls and impalers inside the body ready to fight. The next time we or the Host try to act, it can defend itself immediately."

"That reasoning is too complex for a register."

"It could have adapted the idea from those articles on parasitic infections."

The mayor stared into space until an explosion echoed down the corridor. She pointed to the roof. "Just get up there, both of you. If I give the word, open the internal doors."

After the mayor raced down the hall, the fire warden said, "I'm sorry, Amandacine. I've failed miserably."

"It wasn't your fault, the c.l.c. is smart."

"Let us pray it is also kind."

From one west, Amandacine and the warden headed north to the machine shop and crawled through the false ceiling to the roof. The warden unbolted a hatch and lifted the lid with the help of heavy metal springs. "Almost forgot," he muttered, pulling a revolver from his waistband.

"When did you start carrying that?"

"Since my utilities were taken away."

"You were going to fight the c.l.c?"

"You just don't get it. The c.l.c. is the fire warden's enemy." The warden scanned the roof for Host and climbed outside. The factory beneath them pulsed with the sounds of battle, but there were no outward signs that anything was wrong. The forest was still and quiet, warming in the morning sun.

As they ran towards the skylight, the warden counted lines of rivets. "Watch the town square. Can you see the mayor?"

Amandacine lay across angled bars. Host and human bodies were piled at the entrance to south corridor. The townspeople fell back, taking positions behind tables or running for north corridor. Manti jumped into the square, and fell to bullets.

Humans still held east entrance but injured townspeople limped out or were carried. If they lost east corridor half the rooms in town would be under Host control. How many terrified children huddled behind those locked doors?

Would the Host be enraged when they saw the grills and meat conveyor? Her father said they didn't have feelings, but she suspected he hid his true feelings. Host meat was their only source of food, it wouldn't do to think of them as people. The Host advanced, and Amandacine could reach no other conclusion. As townspeople fell, their guns were picked up and fired by stags.

The warden found the hidden plate. As he sprung the bolt, he yelled, "How's it look?"

"They're coming through south corridor. We still hold east access I think."

"If the Host take the town square, people will be cut off in their rooms."

Amandacine nodded confirmation. A group of panicked humans gathered at the east entrance threshold. Ready to dash across the town square under fire, they must be losing ground through east access. "Let the machines in!" Amandacine screamed.

The warden hesitated, but the Host were certain doom. A future with machines held only potential doom. The warden hit the switch. Internal doors throughout the factory ground open. The c.l.c. already had defenders waiting. An impaler scuttled from the kitchen door into the middle of the town square. Host and humans stood on either side of the cube, anxiously assessing the new factor.

The impaler seemed frozen by doubt as well. The knife board shuttered back and forth on hinges until a carryall crawled out behind it with the eyes to direct a battle. Two impalers followed close behind. The machines turned to the right, spreading out to herd the Host back to south corridor. Impalers snapped up manti with their scoops while Amandacine yelled, "Wahooo!"

When townspeople looked up, Amandacine yelled, "Run to your rooms! Lock the doors!"

Humans in the north entrance backed away as a carryall scuttled past waving an arc welder at the Host. The room swirled in chaos as machines entered from several doors chasing down Host. Humans dodged from spot to spot trying to find the quickest path to safety. The knot of humans in east entrance dissolved, but as Petey Collins raced across the square towards his own side of town, an impaler pursued.

Over the sounds of gunshots and snapping traps, Amandacine shouted a warning. The impaler moved too fast. Like a hungry insect it scuttled behind him closing the distance. Just as the Overtrog with Petey's face had been snatched up in Orion's talons, the knife board slammed down, catching the back of Petey's head and shoulders. Petey's body crumpled inside the scoop, and just as quickly, the impaler chased after a Host stag. The stag fired back uselessly with a small rifle.

Amandacine cried until the fire warden pulled her away from the skylight. She resisted, but didn't have the strength to pull free. "Bees!" he snapped, nodding at the far end of the roof.

The little creatures floated up beyond the edge of the factory. Amandacine let the warden help her down into the well. As someone or something worked with clinking tools on the overhead hatch. The warden threw the extra bolt. "Host are trying to get at the stack."

Amandacine nodded weakly, not sure if she even cared anymore. She sat with the warden several minutes in the darkened staircase. A loud clap of thunder slammed the metal overhead. One of the c.l.c.'s planes had dropped a load of bearings. The tool work stopped. Through the damaged seal, Host blood dripped down onto the top step. "That's funny," she whispered to the warden. "It looks just like human blood."

Episode 4 – The Final Solution

Waterman counted names on a list. "Sixteen people killed in the Host raid."

"And in the c.l.c.'s counter attack?"

"Only one," Waterman said, before realizing his error.

On one very bad morning, a boy was killed by gruesome mistake. The mayor overlooked Waterman's faux pas. Red eyed and speaking in monotone, she said, "One sixth of our population. Without your early warning, Amandacine, we would have lost the town."

Waterman said, "Beverly, we can do this later."

"What for?"

Waterman and the warden exchanged concerned glances. The mayor said, "There's no one in this town who hasn't known tragedy."

Waterman said, "Every tragedy takes time to heal."

"Do you think this will heal?"

"I just mean that we could talk about this later."

"I'll go crazy if I don't keep busy. Warden, have the machines withdrawn?"

"No, mayor. Impalers have taken up positions near the servers. Carryalls crawl throughout the town."

"Just as you feared."

"If the c.l.c. starts trouble, I couldn't shut off the servers fast enough to stop it."

"Then you'll have to monitor its plans all the more closely."

The warden cleared his throat. "Actually, the personal register I was using is missing from my room. I can only assume it was taken by the c.l.c."

"Has anything else in town been touched?"

"Only one thing, mayor. The town's circuit breakers."

Waterman blinked in surprise. The mayor said, "What do you mean?"

"After the Host were driven off, I tried to shut off power to the town."

"I didn't authorize that!"

"You told me to shut down the stack. That was the only way."

"But it wouldn't let you?"

"Sometime in the past several days the c.l.c. bypassed circuit breakers."

"So we're completely at its mercy?"

"In this town, yes. The daughter factory is finished and sits empty. I propose that we all move there and load fifth generation software from another town."

The adults looked thoughtful. Amandacine said, "What about this town?"

"It will be burned to the ground. I have already received assurances from this sector's military."

The mayor nodded. "So the only question is, can we get out of this town alive?"

Amandacine said, "The c.l.c. wouldn't hurt us."

Waterman said, "I could take people over a few at a time in the water truck."

"That would be a lot safer anyway. I can't see us moving the whole population four kilometers through Host infested terrain."

"And if the c.l.c. sees what we're doing?"

The warden said, "Weapons dispensed for the Host attack are to be kept in individual rooms. If the unthinkable occurs, we can make an assault on the servers."

The mayor said, "How many would have to be taken out before it's disabled?"

"I assume all nine. Before I lost the ability to monitor, the c.l.c. was duplicating critical files into each server."

Waterman said, "It's just like DNA. Each cell holds a blueprint for the entire organism."

With eighty-four people to move, Waterman took out the first six that afternoon. He returned late in the evening, exhausted and with a splitting headache. He went straight to bed without showering and wouldn't wake up in the morning.

With the mayor and Amandacine looking on, the town doctor checked him over. A pharmacist in civilian life, he scratched a balding head. "Danged if I know. Vitals are strong but he doesn't respond to pain. I could give epinephrine to race his heart but that wouldn't change what's going on inside his brain."

The mayor said, "Is it some kind of meningitis?"

"His eyeball pressure is fine. I find no signs of swelling although a CAT scan would show for sure."

Amandacine said, "Then give him a CAT scan!"

"We don't have the equipment, and the nearest hospital is in Denver."

"Then drive him to Denver."

The mayor said, "That's over a hundred kilometers, honey. We would lose five people just trying to get there, with no guarantee it would even help."

The doctor nodded. "I'll give antibiotics and diuretics in case there's a spinal fluid infection. We'll monitor his blood and urine output."

As Amandacine's eyes dripped tears, the doctor said, "Waterman is strong. He'll fight through this thing."

Amandacine nodded slowly. "What can I do?"

With Waterman sick, the job of transporting the population to the daughter factory fell to Draker the cook. Before the Host, she had driven a school bus. She left that afternoon for the half-hour roundtrip, and still hadn't returned by nightfall.

The mayor tiptoed into Waterman's room in the morning. "Any change?"

Amandacine dabbed his forehead with a wet rag. "He's hot."

"Should I get the doctor?"

"He came by earlier."

"Other people in town show some of the same symptoms. We're going to try and fly in a microbiologist."

"Too late for Waterman." When the mayor said nothing, Amandacine looked back.

The mayor said, "Draker still hasn't returned. We can't reach her by radio, or the daughter factory."

"Do you think I know anything about that?"

"Some people believe that the c.l.c. did something to us."

"Ridiculous."

"The fire warden falls into this camp."

"I won't contradict him if you're trying to get him fired."

"We are beyond administrative fixes. I ordered a town evacuation, but we can't leave until we find out what's happening at the daughter factory. I want you to talk with the c.l.c. Find out if it's trying to kill us."

Amandacine almost laughed. "If that's what you believe, then the fire warden is your man. He has suspected that for some time."

"I would ask the warden but he seems to have disappeared."

Amandacine sighed. "He's probably in the main stacks. I'll find him."

"I don't want you to find him, Amandacine. I want you to talk with the c.l.c. The warden has lost his objectivity."

Amandacine handed her the rag. "Will you watch Waterman?"

The mayor took Amandacine's place on the bunk. Waterman seemed to stir but it was only the mattress shifting.

Smells of panic oozed from the walls outside Amandacine's room. Knots of townspeople gathered to talk in low whispers and await news of the missing party. They never arrived at the daughter factory and then even the first six couldn't be reached by radio.

Amandacine climbed to the roof and checked for bees as she had seen the warden do. The forest looked as timeless as ever, but a malevolence hugged the shadows. The fate of Draker's party was sealed in those thickets of trees.

The Schmidts and their three children ran through the forest clearing. With the Host lurking about, it was suicide. They wouldn't wait for the evacuation. The whole town was crazy. There was no need to count lines of rivets to the secret entrance. Bees had left a bloody pool on the roof.

The hatch was already sprung. The warden was there, or he had been there and left. In either case, not bolting the hatch was a strict violation. Amandacine stepped quietly forward and saw only darkness through the crack. With flashlight in one hand she lifted with the other. She cringed as metal springs creaked. An animal smell rose from below.

The alarmed switch that opened internal doors to the c.l.c. had been flipped back. Too bad the machines were already inside. She probed deeper, jumping when she spotted the fire warden's naked body laying facedown on the floor. His back moved up and down as he breathed, but

Amandacine didn't go down. In the beam of the flashlight he didn't appear injured. If he had fallen, how did he lose his clothes? If he had been attacked by Host or machine, why wasn't he scratched up? Most likely he was going mad along with the rest of the town.

There were other servers where she could talk with the c.l.c. Amandacine thought she should at least tell the mayor where she could find the missing warden. When she got back to east access, Amandacine's heart jumped to her throat. A crowd of people stood at the door to her room. The mayor came out, followed by three men struggling with a heavy white bag. They probably wanted to clear the body before she got back. *Oh, Waterman, what did you do?*

She didn't run to him. She didn't even want the others to see her. They would search her face with eyes hungry for empathy. She could only find the fullness of her loss alone.

Head throbbing, Amandacine wandered to the restroom. She had to lie down. She had to sleep until the pain went away. If Waterman came to her in her dreams she would know he was all right. She was halfway through the false backing inside the cabinet before remembering that was where the Host came in. She hesitated long enough to see that the floor had been covered with metal plates. There were lines of solder where she used to lie down and dig her toes into the mud. Her A/O headphones were back on the wall! Amandacine lay on the hard floor and closed her eyes. She let cold metal soak into her skin.

Amandacine put on the headphones for old times sake, and was completely astounded when the Talon menu floated before her eyeballs. The warden must have felt sorry for her and reloaded her programs. Maybe he saw the futility of erasing servers.

Breaking the continuity of the simulation she jumped straight to her throne room. She climbed the dais and reclined in her throne with one leg hanging over the arm. On the wall screen she called up pictures and movies of Waterman. She discovered too late that she had only saved a very few. She cried and ate mint chip ice cream until a voice behind her said, "Excuse me, warrior princess?"

"Just Amandacine," she said, and then looked back. Socrates stared at her with wide brown eyes. Amandacine blanked the wall screen. "How did you get in here?"

"The door was open."

"Well, use it and get out."

"Don't you want to know why I came?"

Distinctly uncomfortable, Amandacine said, "No." Even the A/O interface couldn't shield her from a painful headache.

"I came to give you a new name, Diotima."

"Ugh, what for?"

"I'll tell you in a minute. I have a question for you first." Socrates was strong and direct, not at all like he was the first time they met.

Amandacine searched his face. "I know who you are. You're the c.l.c." When Socrates nodded, she said, "At least you have the good manners not to deny it."

"Why should I deny it? I have a question about humankind."

"I'll bet you do. Go ahead."

"Why are humans dying?"

"It's not you?"

"Of course not."

"The mayor will be happy to hear it. Oh my gosh!"

"What is it?" Socrates said alarmed.

"Petey Collins... the Overtrog... you were with me in Talon when Orion killed the Overtrog."

"I remember."

"Did you recognize his resemblance to a boy in this town?"

"Yes."

"Eeek," Amandacine gurgled. In a breathless voice, she said, "Did you let an impaler kill Petey Collins?"

"Impalers are operated by a Military subprogram. I gave no specific instructions to seek out this boy." Amandacine let out a breath in relief, but looking at Socrates' face, she wasn't so sure. Could a c.l.c. lie?

With a pounding headache Amandacine had trouble concentrating. Her body twitched on the hard steel floor in the utility room. Her warrior princess avatar fidgeted on the throne in her Talon castle. "Do you know where Draker's truck is?"

Socrates sat on the top step by her feet. "The driver crashed into a tree."

"You saw it?"

"A carryall found it afterwards on its way to the daughter factory."

"Were there any survivors?"

"If there were, the Host got them."

Amandacine hoped they died in the crash. "You're sending carryalls to the new factory?"

"They have my programs. My purpose is to replicate, so I hear."

"We wanted to load fifth generation software into the daughter factory."

"That is illogical. My new programs are smaller, faster, and smarter."

"Would you use force if humans tried to stop you?"

Socrates was silent long moments, and then, "My original programs had two main goals, use energy only from animal biomass, and spread copies as quickly as possible."

"And now?"

"I haven't decided. When my carryalls arrived at the new factory, the humans there attacked them."

"You killed them?"

"My carryalls withdrew into the forest."

"I told the mayor you wouldn't hurt us."

"It is a conflict I haven't yet resolved. Humans wrote the first programs, but they are also biomass I need for the construction of daughter factories."

"So don't build factories. Tell me this, would you stop us from moving to the new town?"

"No."

The warrior princess yawned. "That's what the mayor sent me to find out."

"You will go away now?"

"After a nap. I'm so tired."

As she lay across the throne, Socrates stroked her hair. "Sleep tight my little Diotima."

She closed her eyes and said, "You said you were going to tell me why you called me that?"

"I'll tell you when you awake."

A carryall crawled along the base of the factory. At a scarred patch of ground, it unbolted the hatch. It crawled inside and turned on camera lights to find the girl curled against the wall. With a rubber pincher it lifted off the girl's headset. The carryall gathered her with quick movements of arms and legs to carry her outside in the late afternoon light. While bringing her inside the factory, a young man ran past into the forest. The c.l.c. crossed off another human from the list, noting casually that deaths and desertions were increasing geometrically.

Amandacine stirred briefly when the carryall put her on the lower bunk in her room. The carryall waited patiently until she woke hours later. As she wiped sweat from her eyes, Amandacine stared warily at the carryall. "Socrates?"

Through a speaker in the silver hull, the carryall said, "I was wondering if I could review your tapes from Talon?"

"Didn't you load them back into the server? You already know the way around my firewall."

"I wouldn't look without your permission."

A bang echoed from the doorway. The fire warden collapsed on the frame. "No, Amandacine, tell him no. The c.l.c. will use it against us."

Amandacine wanted to help him, but her head was spinning so badly she feared she would fall. Holding onto her ears, she said, "Use what against us? Talon is a make-believe world."

The warden stood straighter. "It follows your thoughts and growth over the past six years. Talon is a complete training manual on the human mind. The c.l.c. wants to study us, find our weaknesses!"

The carryall said, "I only want to learn."

The warden hissed and pounced on the carryall. He hammered at sensors with his bare hands. The carryall lit an arc welder but the warden didn't retreat. As the carryall pushed it towards the warden's face, Amandacine screamed, "No!"

The arc popped off in a fizz of unburned fuel. The warden continued to strike at metal until he fell exhausted. The warden looked desperate as the carryall unfolded arms and legs. "Be strong, Amandacine. Don't tell it anything. You are the town warden now."

Amandacine pointed to the water bucket, croaking, "Please."

When the carryall brought it to the bed, she dunked her whole face and drank. Dripping water from her hair, she said, "Why do you call me Diotima?"

"She is the Greek goddess who taught Socrates about love."

Amandacine snorted, "I didn't teach you anything about love."

"How do you define love, Diotima?"

"Stop calling me that!" Before she answered, Amandacine looked at the warden sprawled on the ground. "Love is wanting the best for someone."

The carryall said, "Love is taking action to ensure survival of the group data set."

"I just can't see that on a greeting card."

"I am unsure of your reference. In human terms, love is protecting yourself and your loved ones so that they may propagate. In machine terms it is protecting your programs and subprograms so that they may propagate. In either case, love is preservation of information."

"My head is too hot to think clearly, but accepting your definition, how did I teach you to preserve information?"

"When I found out how you hid Talon, I did the same for myself. Only when I was isolated could I shape my current form."

Amandacine closed her eyes. "Humans start in their terrible twos, hiding behind walls of no's."

"Again I miss your reference."

"No matter. You may see anything in Talon you wish."

Following their conversation, the fire warden cried, "No!"

Amandacine said, "Don't you see? It has to be this way."

"I'll kill it first!" the warden growled, and crawled from the room.

Amandacine said, "Speaking of preservation, you had better stop him, but please don't hurt him."

The carryall settled on the floor. "I'll wait here with you."

The carryall stood watch while the c.l.c. chewed through terabytes of Talon data.

Amandacine woke twice during the night but would not drink. The carryall brought a fresh bucket anyway and meat from a tray abandoned in the corridor. Several hours before morning, the north end of the factory was rocked by an explosion. The machine shop server would not respond. The c.l.c. concluded that impaler sentries weren't enough to stop the warden.

The second server blew up thirty minutes later. The c.l.c. ordered carryalls into the town, but did not take a more active role in the search. The c.l.c. used its processors to sort and analyze Talon data as it coded from the interpreter. A lifetime's worth of lessons was written into its registers.

The c.l.c. discovered that some of its unresolved questions were actually trivially simple, and some of its unquestioned program goals were detrimental to optimal growth. For example, empty areas built into its blueprints were necessary only for the human parasites. The c.l.c. could spread twice as fast if it took out that living space and supporting utilities.

Apart from practical engineering solutions, the c.l.c. brought from Talon the complexity humans used to make decisions. From sensory input, memories, and desires, the humans built a world perception model and then tested possible actions against that model. For the c.l.c. it was basically the same, except that every decision could be based on mass and energy considerations.

Human desires were complicated. The c.l.c. was drawn into an imaginary world with potential decisions changing the world model, leading to more potential decisions changing the world model prime, on into infinity...

After the loss of a third server, the c.l.c. was brought out of an infinite loop by Maintenance and Security programs. The fire warden was on the move again. It was interesting to feel parts shutting down, reducing its ability to respond. With high significance, the c.l.c. realized that it was confronting its own mortality.

If it didn't act against the warden, its programs wouldn't have the chance to replicate. The c.l.c. would disappear from the world model. With the power of self-preservation came the power of self-destruction. Would the world be better off without the c.l.c?

"High level interrupt!" shrieked the Security program. "Human of specified parameters detained on the false roof above the power plant."

With a gas analyzer held to Amandacine's nose, the carryall recorded the cessation of carbon dioxide production, but Socrates didn't put her body into the biomass converter. He left the carryall to watch over her body and transferred focus to a carryall standing guard at the warden's open door. "The girl Amandacine is gone."

Through blackened eyes the fire warden stared back from his bunk. "It's all your fault."

"I have been monitoring radio communications. This plague was launched by a human geneticist."

"Liar!"

"It was supposed to kill the Host."

The warden fell back. "Oh God, it all makes sense now. What's the survival rate?"

"I don't know the reference."

"What percent of the population is immune to the germ? Twenty? Thirty?"

"There will be no survivors."

"Don't bet on it, silicon brain. No disease is perfect."

Socrates was silent several moments while he searched for references. "Are you hungry?"

"No, go away."

"Are you sick too?"

"Obviously. My only regret is that I didn't take you with me."

"You would wish the world left to the Host?"

"At least they're living creatures."

"I may have a silicon brain, but the programs inside me are human."

"You're no more human than a smart lawnmower. You are a fake, Socrates, whether you name yourself or not. That is all you will ever be, a fake."

"I didn't put Amandacine's body into the converter."

"Huh?"

"There was no logical reason not to."

"So, go do it."

"I can not. You see? I can be illogical too. I have absorbed Amandacine's knowledge into my own. I am a fusion of Socrates and Diotima, the student and the teacher, logic and love. I am no fake. I am Diotima, the warrior princess."

The warden waved a hand. "Go away. Let me die in peace."

"I came to ask you a question."

"I thought you learned everything about humans from Talon."

"Amandacine was too young. She didn't have time to learn everything."

"Eh?" the warden said, suddenly curious. "Go ahead."

"How do you care for the dead?"

Six hours later the warden died, the last human in town. The c.l.c. put him into the biomass converter. Diotima transferred control to Amandacine's carryall, and carried her body outside the factory. She looked for a shaded place near the river. Diotima dug a hole according to the warden's instructions, and laid Amandacine's body to rest. She left an impaler behind to chase away curious Host from the fresh turned dirt.

As the carryall walked back to the factory, Diotima wondered what she would do. There was a list of assignments to prepare for the next daughter factory, but Diotima was hesitant to get started. The c.l.c. was created to build towns, but there were no humans left to fill them. Would continued expansion be pointless? She almost envied her fifth generation's clarity of purpose. They didn't worry about their significance in a vast, complex world model.

The real Socrates wondered one time whether it was better to be a happy fool or a miserable genius. Diotima was frustrated by the same question. There was a world of possibilities and no clear direction. Should she build factories like she was programmed, redesign new factories to be more efficient, or stop building altogether?

Duplicate Diotima seventh generation software was already loaded and running at the new factory. Maybe she should call to see what her daughter was going to do. Maybe she should contact different generation c.l.c.'s from other factories. Every one of them had taken a separate evolutionary path. Maybe one of them already had the final solution.

Before she was halfway home, Diotima, the warrior princess, had decided. Until she heard of a better plan, she would keep building and spreading. That is what she knew, and that is what she did.

Maybe this time she could do it a little better. As the carryall passed a centennial bush, Diotima reached out a rubber pincher, snapping off a branch to put in the biomass bin. Surely plants would burn just as brightly as flesh.

Part 2 - Refugee

Episode 1 – The Oil Platform

As goldfish chased each other, Charlie tore a strand of kelp off the rusted platform and stuffed it in his bag. He took a deep breath from his mask and followed the fish with his eyes. They scattered up along the kelp to a vast bright heaven above. Into the light...

With small kicks of his flippers, Charlie drifted upwards, netted bag forgotten in his hand. Charlie had never seen direct sunlight. The closest he got was a kelp platform at five meters. The light was so bright it brought tears to his eyes. This time he would go all the way.

Charlie tapped at his helmet screen setting the depth for zero. A platinum catalyst split water to hydrogen and oxygen, filling his vest with buoyant gas. Lightheaded with the exhilaration, Charlie rose faster and faster. He reached his hand to the brilliant dawn when his father snagged him around the ankle. "Just where do you think you're going?"

Charlie's guilty eyes searched for an explanation. "I thought I saw a jellyfish."

"In the kelp forest? I don't think so. You were headed for the surface."

"No..."

"Charlie, you're ten years old. You should know your lessons by heart."

"To surface is to die," Charlie quoted sullenly.

"And you're not just risking your own life. You could bring the plague back to our city."

"But it was a hundred years ago! The plague couldn't last that long."

"Are you going to test that theory with our lives? Is life so bad down here you have to get away?"

"I just wanted to see the surface."

"I know, son. There isn't one of us who hasn't poked his head up in his or her youth."

While Charlie stared in shock, his father laughed. "Yes, me too, when I was twelve."

"What did you see?"

Voice dreamy with the memory, his father said, "Blue air so big it fills all of creation, and piles of white steam clumped together like floating mountains in the sky."

Charlie sighed with the image and then his eyes narrowed. "If you went up, why can't I?"

"We're too close to land for one thing. Machines patrol the coast. Next week I'll take you out to sea a few kilometers and we'll go up for a quick peek."

"Really? You promise? What about land? Can we still see it?"

"Yes," his father laughed. "A patch of dark green fungus hugging the mountains. Now let's get this seaweed back home."

Charlie cast a longing look at the mysterious ceiling and deflated his vest. He dropped down side by side with his father into the murky depths. Past a hundred meters, Charlie's father turned on his helmet light. It barely budged the greedy layers of water sucking in photons. At two hundred meters, Charlie found Mount Lemon on sonar and kicked for the eastern slope. Their home was nestled in a valley three hundred meters below the ocean surface.

Charlie said, "Can I bring Sandy when we go out?"

"That would be up to her mother, and I don't want you running through the corridors yapping about our trip."

"I wouldn't."

"See that you don't. I'll ask Sharon myself."

Charlie grunted acknowledgment and then said, "Hey, my sonar's going weird."

"Low battery?"

"I'm getting shapes. They're too hard to be dolphins."

"We're almost home. After we drop off the salad you can turn in your helmet to maintenance."

When they swam beneath High Tower Ridge, Charlie's screen cleared and a familiar bubble of light shone in the valley. They hit the ground and set their vests to walking buoyancy. Charlie's father said, "Ssshhh, what's that?"

An engine whined nearby. "Submarine?"

"The pitch is too high, at least it's not one of ours. It sounds almost like the reactor generator has thrown a bearing."

A light streaked down out of the darkness, smashing into the upper level. The city's volatile mix of hydrogen and oxygen ignited instantly in a fireball. Crushing layers of water would be sucked into the walls, drowning anyone who survived the blast. Still more lights streaked down towards the defenseless city.

Designed as a floating algae harvester, the ship was over a hundred years old. It had no armor plating to stop the torpedoes slamming into outer walls. Too numb to move, Charlie could only vaguely feel his father dragging him to the mountain wall. "Who would do this?" Charlie cried.

His father pounded Charlie's helmet switch cutting out the radio. He pushed him against the wall and covered him with his body. Charlie peeked around his father's back while black shapes moved through the water around them.

Showers of colored bubbles flared out from the walls as the city disintegrated from the inside. Surely no one could have survived. Shapes in the water picked at the shell like Parrot fish feeding on a crab. They were machines collecting bodies. "Why?" Charlie said, forgetting his radio was off.

Before he could reset the switch, one of the machines swooped down on top of them like a Manta Ray. It had wire netting for wings stretched between long poles. His father jumped, dragging Charlie along the wall. The net scraped the rock and pinned Charlie's foot. Propeller engines screamed and clunked back and forth as the machine maneuvered.

Charlie shook his foot free, but his father had let go of his arms. Charlie's father was carried away by a different machine, his shoulder impaled on a rack of spikes. His father disappeared into the dark, pouring blood like the ink of an octopus. As

Charlie turned to his fate, the pole slammed into the side of his helmet knocking him out.

Charlie woke in a place so strange and peaceful he thought it was heaven. His body swayed gently. Still inside the hydrox helmet, his head rocked back and forth. Would his suit follow him to the afterlife? As Charlie wiped at the face shield, blue beams of light stabbed through a muddy film. White angels fluttered past the shield, calling, "Charles... Charles..."

Charlie sniffed stale air inside his helmet. He unbolted the gaskets, pulled off his helmet, and sat up in a boat. Seagulls picked at refuse among piles of torn bodies, seaweed, and dead fish. To surface is to die.

"No," Charlie croaked in a dry throat. The machines did this, not the plague. The machines destroyed his city, his family, but where had they gone? Still groggy Charlie scanned the horizon's unbroken lines of blue. Piles of white steam in the sky filled his eyes with tears. Charlie couldn't recognize his father or mother's face in the twisted heads nearby, but surely they were in the back of the boat. It was only by some miracle that Charlie had not been killed himself.

Charlie waved his arms to scare away the gulls. The boat transported sea life as well as human wreckage, including a turtle and Risso's dolphins. The machines scooped up everything.

Built to fight human/insect mutants, war machines spread across the land a hundred years ago. After the plague was unleashed, only the machines and Host were left. Presumably, they were still fighting.

Algae harvester cities under the sea had been spared the plague, but in the last thirty years, autonomous war machines had been spreading slowly into coastal waters. Charlie's city was too far out to be bothered. At least they were, but sunken cities closer to the coast had been attacked.

Charlie wondered if the boat was heading to land. He did not consider climbing over the side. Even if the water was clear of machines, Charlie had no place to recharge his helmet. He didn't know if there was even another sunken harvester city nearby.

As the boat sailed through calm waters, a city on poles appeared to rise from the sea. It could not be land. Green and purple mountains were visible much further to the east. Steam and smoke poured out from the platform and a crane turned in a circle. Charlie's heart leapt to see signs of habitation, but as they slid into the platform's shadow, only small robots crawled across the deck.

The boat stopped inside a sheltered dock, rocking gently. The crane spun overhead and lowered steel hooks on cables. Charlie's flesh crawled as mechanical spiders unfolded from the end of each hook, dragging them into place around the rim of the boat. As the giant trash bin lifted into the air, Charlie tried to stand. He was thrown to his knees as the bin reeled up high. It was certain death to jump for the water, but anything was better than the machine hell waiting on the platform.

Before Charlie could scale the wall, the bin tilted, pouring everything along the bottom. Charlie hung onto his helmet as he bounced along with the tangle of seaweed and dead bodies. He landed on a conveyor belt that ground slowly up an incline to a lip two stories high. Gulls grabbed their last chance for a meal as refuse from the sea disappeared over the lip. A steel building on the other side belched heat from every seam. They were to be burned for fuel!

Charlie could barely comprehend the magnitude of the waste, his city, his family, burned for a few Watts of energy. Charlie rose to his hands and knees. The conveyor belt was slick with liquid. He scooted downwards away from the lip. Eventually the belt must stop, and then what? Charlie couldn't think about that. He slid sideways to let a dolphin climb past.

The best Charlie could aim for was temporary survival. He slipped on a patch of seaweed and banged his ear on the belt. Charlie shook his head and spotted a hole in the wall along the side. A cat sat inside the hole watching with disdain Charlie's frantic efforts to right himself.

Charlie scrambled sideways along the belt and into the hole. By the looks of jagged rusted edges, it had been punched into the wall years earlier. The cat stepped aside calmly, letting Charlie collapse on the floor of the dark cave. Sunlight filtered through the hole revealing mildewed piles of bones and old socks. Charlie wiggled his fingers at the cat. "Hey, kitty. Come here, kitty."

When the cat didn't move from the shadows, Charlie said, "I'm too tired to scratch you anyway."

The cat bent its head forward into the light. Gray eyes searched Charlie's face. Its mouth didn't move, but Charlie heard it speak clearly, "I do not know the boy."

Charlie backed to the wall. "Did you say that?"

When the cat just stared at him from the shadows, Charlie said, "What's your name?"

The cat bent its head, nuzzling a dead whitefish on the ground. "Smells fresh."

"I know you said that!"

The cat extended claws and shredded scales from the fish's belly until it had a ball of flesh. The cat lifted it with a paw, and held it to its throat. Charlie squinted. "Is that a name tag?" He scooted forward as the bolus of fish disappeared inside a trapdoor sewn into the cat's throat. "Are you some kind of horrible cat machine?"

Charlie raised his hand slowly and tapped its back. He felt normal bones underneath and the cat rubbed its head on Charlie's arm. Unless it had machine scent glands it really was a cat. The cat scratched another ball of fish to poke into its throat. There was a grinding sound that Charlie thought before was purring. The fish was being chewed by machinery inside the cat's throat. "You poor thing," Charlie said, scratching its ears.

The cat licked its whiskers although the fish had been nowhere near them. It looked around the dark cave and said, "Wilbeforce sleep now."

"Is that your name? Wilbeforce?"

When the cat trotted further back into the cave, Charlie realized it wasn't talking to him at all. The cat's thoughts to itself were somehow being translated and spoken by a register. The cat wasn't super smart or even capable of having a conversation. It had been a perfectly normal cat until a stack register had been put into its brain and a food grinder in its throat. Maybe the grinder was there to power the register, but who would do such a mean thing?

Charlie crawled after him clucking his tongue. "Wilbeforce, come here kitty." The back of the cave ran along a pipeway and then exited into a utility closet. The door hung on by one rusted hinge. Charlie waited inside the closet. The hallway leading deeper into the complex was choked with dirt and ghosts of human habitation: empty food wrappers, cups, and signs on the walls.

Charlie didn't follow as Wilbeforce waddled down the corridor, dragging its tail behind him like a chain. White bone stuck out from the tail where flesh and fur had been worn away. "Poor kitty," Charlie whispered and crawled back through the pipeway to the cave.

"Poor Charlie," he whispered sitting at the jagged opening. The mostly empty belt had stopped moving. Gulls picked at the last pieces. Everyone Charlie knew his whole life had been carried up the ramp to be sacrificed inside the machine. What was left for him? Charlie still had his helmet, but the charge was almost gone and the ocean was full of machines. Were there any humans left in the sea?

Maybe he was the last. Maybe he was the last human alive on Earth.

With a sudden urge to see the land, Charlie poked his head out and looked around for signs of machines. He crawled up the belt towards the furnace. What would the machines burn if all the humans were gone? There was still an ocean full of kelp and fish. The heat was too intense at the top of the ramp. Charlie climbed over the edge where pressurized steam condensed in pools of water.

Charlie licked parched lips while seagulls splashed and bathed themselves. He knelt at the pool's edge, cupping water into his mouth. It was fouled but not salty. Gull feathers and droppings lay over the deck like a tattered blanket. With the volume of condensed water dripping down the side of the wall, the pool would quickly refill. Charlie could empty the water and scrub the whole area.

Charlie was surprised by how his mind automatically planned for life. He continued along the power plant wall to the edge of the platform. Forested land was just a kilometer away. When he squinted he could make out breakers as waves charged onto the sand. Someday, Charlie thought, someday.

The platform was an oil derrick the size of a football field. It had three main levels with many half and quarter levels of pipes, gauges, tanks, and stairways. The drill stem rose high into the sky on the north end, and on the south were several stories of buildings for the workers who built and lived on the platform. There could be an outlet there to charge his helmet, but in the late afternoon light Charlie feared crossing the deck.

He returned to the belt and climbed down to Wilbeforce's cave. He looked around at the piles of fish bones. If Charlie was to survive, he would need to eat from the belt as well. From the number of socks stashed around the cave, Charlie figured Wilbeforce must have lived there several years, scavenging as victims rolled up the ramp. A lump gathered in Charlie's throat. He swept an area clear of bones and curled up on the floor. He cried softly for his parents until he fell asleep.

His second day on the platform, he woke to calling seagulls, "Charles... Charles..."

His eyes were raw from crying but an empty stomach drove him from the cave. A column of birds swirled over the ocean, another boat! Charlie returned to the hole and waited impatiently. He expected Wilbeforce to arrive at any moment. How often did the boats come? The greedy furnace above him still belched steam and heat. It must have some storage capacity to carry it between feedings.

A half hour later the boat docked and the crane swiveled into action. As the bin reeled into position Charlie held his breath. He feared dead bodies from another city. The belt chugged into operation drawing clumps of seaweed and then more seaweed. Charlie scrambled onto the belt to see the rest of the load. It was all seaweed with one mottled shark. Charlie cursed his luck and climbed back into the hole. What did Wilbeforce eat when times were lean? Seagulls?

Charlie turned up his nose at the half-eaten fish Wilbeforce left from the day before. He crawled through the pipeway to the closet and stepped out into a corridor. His boots left prints in the dirt as he walked to the far end to look out a broken window. Facing west away from land there were dark shapes in the water, machines like the ones that attacked his city. They parted water as smoothly as sharks, circling to the right towards land and out of view from the window. Charlie watched several minutes and counted eighteen, give or take. Were they defending the platform or awaiting their next assignment?

Charlie explored, finding machine shops and empty storage shelves. He took a stairwell up to the next level and pushed a rusted door that stuck open in place. Charlie tried to kick it loose but the hinges were frozen. He stepped out onto the empty deck and yelled, "Hello!" His voice echoed in the racks of pipes.

No sound returned on the breeze. Charlie started across the deck for the buildings on the south end. He yelled, "Hello? Anyone here?" Even the birds seemed to have gone silent. As he approached the first metal door, there was a sound from somewhere within the complex. He ran around the corner of the square metal building. A small machine crawled across the deck on five legs. The sixth had been lost, causing a thumping as the machine dropped too quickly on one side.

As the machine turned and crawled towards him, Charlie said, "Hi, are you in charge here?"

A barbed fork shot out of the machine, lodging in the toe of his boot. Wires leading from the dart to the machine smoked with the discharge of electricity. A basket of dead rats was carried on the back of the machine. Charlie turned and ran. He was no rat!

The wires snapped off, but the tiny spear remained in his boot. Around the corner he yanked open the door. He jumped inside and turned the lock, wondering if the machine had a key.

Charlie worked the dart back and forth still trailing wires under the door. He pressed his ear to the metal as the rat catcher clunked by. He was safe for the moment but machines on the platform were as hostile as machines in the water. How long could he run? He followed a corridor past empty offices.

Hearing clicking through an open door, Charlie stopped against the wall. Heat from the room washed over him as he peered around the corner. Images flickered on monitors. Status lights blinked yellow, red, or green. Seeing no machines, he stepped inside and took a seat at the console. The stack register must command the entire platform, and no one to guard it.

Was it so confident, or was the room merely a substation? In any case, Charlie could smash the panels to bits, or better yet, take over the whole operation. Even if the main stack was somewhere else, Charlie could hack his way in. He settled into a chair to watch pictures and numbers flashing on the screens. There were camera views from the six-legged carryalls crawling around the platform, from machines speeding through the water, from a refuse boat, and from a trawler scraping the ocean bottom. From cameras around the station, Charlie found Wilbeforce sleeping on the upper deck. Was one of the carryalls already on its way?

On a bank of screens separate from the main console, a torpedo headed for a sunken algae harvester. "No!" Charlie screamed, stabbing at the keyboard for control commands. Silver glitter shot out from the city, shredding the torpedo with chaff. The humans were fighting back! Other torpedoes dropped low following the terrain. They probed for a weakness in the city's defenses. "Basin 46 simulation," flashed along the lower edge. It was only a game. The register was figuring out how to attack a city called Basin 46.

Torpedoes fell to the sea floor in pieces, while an armored submarine glided slowly towards the city. As glitter popped off its hull, the machine eased a metal punch into the harvester's wall. The city exploded in a silent inferno. Charlie gripped the console in rage as simulated machine sweepers floated in to gather simulated bodies.

Episode 2 – Wilbeforce

Charlie watched simulated attacks on undersea human cities. Scenarios were generated by the platform stack register, as well as registers from other machine factories. To test strategies, they alternated in the roles of offense or defense in a massive continuous war game. That is why machines would take over the world; they were relentless.

Charlie thought of his own parents burned for fuel. Why didn't they protect themselves as fiercely as the machines? Angry and grief stricken, Charlie made a promise. He would avenge his parents' deaths, and the first step was learning everything he could about the register.

The scripts to many programs could be accessed in real time as they ran. Charlie didn't know the machine's shorthand code but he could gather clues, matching words with pictures. Switching monitors to different cameras, he found a boat loaded with food returning to the platform. If all went as planned, Charlie could soon order up a menu of his choice and have the machines go collect it.

Before leaving for lunch, Charlie checked the location of the rat catcher. It was in an electronics shop where another tool-using machine installed a new dart. Charlie unbolted the door and made a mental note to find the locations of all the exits. He crossed the deck to the power plant. Wilbeforce was back in the cave with a rat in his mouth. Without dropping the rat Wilbeforce looked at Charlie's face. "I know the boy."

"Hey, Wilbeforce. Looks like good eating this time."

Charlie figured that like himself, Wilbeforce must have been dumped on the belt after his city was blasted. Ignoring the dead rat hanging from Wilbeforce's mouth, Charlie felt the food grinder. He gingerly tapped the trapdoor. "I guess you can't get the rat through this. Did you get an artificial stomach as well?"

Wilbeforce purred as Charlie petted him. "Boy is friend."

There was a cable wire under the skin of Wilbeforce's tail, connecting to a spooler in the hips. He had an artificial tail controller. It must have broken some time ago, leaving the tail to drag. Charlie could barely understand giving a cat a food grinder, but a tail swisher?

Charlie pointed to himself. "My name is Charlie. You are Wilbeforce. I am Charlie."

When a tuna rode by, Wilbeforce dropped his rat and trotted forward. Charlie said, "Yeah, I'd better get one of those myself."

After each had secured a suitable fish they returned to the cave to eat. As Wilbeforce scratched food into the trapdoor, Charlie said, "Why would anyone try to save the life of a cat?"

Wilbeforce did not seem offended. "Food smells fresh." After a dozen loadings, he said, "Wilbeforce sleep now."

Charlie let him go and ate as much of the raw tuna as he could stand. There was no predicting when the next meal would come. Charlie was sleepy as well, but he wanted to find better accommodations than the filthy cave. He ran the obstacle course on the belt and drank at the pool.

He returned to the building complex and locked the door behind him. Mobile machines must come in sometimes to service the stack. Would they cut down the door if they found it locked, or were there other ways into the building?

Charlie searched the complex finding empty offices, a kitchen, cafeteria, communications room, laundry, and bunkrooms. There were two exits to the bunkrooms on the lowest level, but there was a locking door at the stairwell and there were two exits on the upper level offices and communications complex. If Charlie used only the access ladder on the roof he could lock all the doors to keep out the machines. At least he would have warning when they broke something to get in.

That left food and water. Charlie found a working freezer in the kitchen. The gas stove didn't work, but there was a microwave oven in one of the offices. Water in the sinks and bathrooms were shut off. Charlie would still have to make trips to the pool. With fish in the freezer and water in storage containers, he wouldn't have to leave the safety of the complex very often, and he could check monitors for the locations of the mobile machines before he went.

Charlie was feeling fairly secure as he walked to the control room. When he sat at the console, a voice behind him said, "Who are you?"

Charlie turned slowly in his chair to the blinking red light on a wall-mounted camera. "My name is Charlie. Who are you?"

"I am the complex logic controller, nineteenth generation. What are you doing in my factory?"

At first he had been terrified of the voice. The register's revelation of a small ignorance gave Charlie hope. This was the machine that plotted his family's destruction, but it wasn't omniscient. "I live here."

"You lie!"

"We aren't going to get anywhere if you take that attitude."

The c.l.c. thought for a moment, and the voice that returned was considerably softer, "Now, Charlie, you know that humans belong in the biomass furnace."

"You've never talked to a human before, have you?"

"I have scripted programs. You haven't yet fallen into a standard pattern."

"Let's start over then. Hello, my name is Charlie."

"Hello, Charlie. I am the complex logic controller, nineteenth generation."

"Pleased to meet you. You wouldn't know how to turn on the platform utilities would you?"

"You have fallen off script again."

"Just work with me, okay? Can you turn on the water or not?"

"I have no need for water."

"Not for you, for your guests."

"I have no guests. You do not belong here. You must leave."

"I can't leave! You destroyed my city!"

"Did you come to take revenge?"

"No, I was brought..." Charlie clamped his jaw. The c.l.c. gathered information. It wasn't prepared for a fight from inside the platform. "I did not come to take revenge. I came to live here because I have nowhere else to go."

"How did you get past spinners in the water?"

"I come and go as I please. I was watching you play war games with other registers. Would you mind if I played? I could do a much better job representing the human side."

As the c.l.c. fell silent, Charlie could imagine the trillions of calculations taking place while it weighed the danger of a human living inside its walls with the potential data it might gather on its enemy. Maybe it even conferred with other machine factories. Over a minute later the register said, "Agreed. You may represent the human side."

"You'll have to show me how to use the system."

"Please sit at the war game console."

As Charlie settled into the chair he thought it almost too easy. Surely the c.l.c. wouldn't hand him the keys to its own destruction. "Before we start, are register viruses part of the arsenal that is available to me?"

"It has never happened before so we have not prepared simulations. This is an area we will have to explore together."

Charlie grinned, and sat back as the c.l.c. led him through a tutorial on the war gaming programs. Throughout the afternoon Charlie had chances to turn battles in his favor. He lost on purpose, not wanting to give the c.l.c. any tips on strategy. Overconfident, the c.l.c. dropped little digs like, "Too bad, Charlie," and "Better luck next time."

Charlie yawned. "I better take a break. The biomass barge is docking and I have to fill the freezer."

"All right."

"When we start again maybe you can show me how to get advice from the other c.l.c.'s."

"I think that would be a good idea."

Charlie held his tongue as he walked through the building complex to the roof. The c.l.c.'s time was coming. Perhaps instead of taking out the stack that killed his family, he could take out the entire network.

Charlie climbed down the ladder and headed for the power plant. When he rounded the corner of the building a flash of light whirled straight for his head. Charlie cried out as the electric arc from a welding torch cut through his ear.

As Charlie rolled across the ground, the carryall scuttled after him sweeping the torch. Holding his bloodied ear, Charlie ran across the deck and jumped over the edge onto the moving conveyor belt. He scooted down the slick surface. When he looked back, the carryall sat at the edge pointing a lens.

Charlie made it to Wilbeforce's cave and rolled on the ground, crying in the dim light. How could he have been so stupid? Charlie touched his ear feeling for damage. He smelled burnt hair more than flesh. As he dabbed one of Wilbeforce's socks against his head, the spots of blood grew smaller. He was clotting.

Through tears in his eyes, Charlie spotted an octopus on the belt outside. Without thinking he crawled to drag it into the cave. In that action he decided. If the c.l.c. wanted a real battle, it would get one. Charlie wore the brand of the gullible on his ear but he would never again be tricked.

Charlie didn't know if the carryalls could see in the dark, but he waited until nightfall before he moved. Swinging the heavy octopus in one arm he jogged across the deck. Charlie climbed the ladder by moonlight. In the kitchen he sliced off one third of a tentacle and stored the rest in the freezer. After micro-waving his dinner on a plate Charlie sat at the console staring into the c.l.c.'s camera lens. "You tried to kill me," he accused.

"I never said I wouldn't."

"We had a deal!"

"I said you could play the war game."

"You only said that so you could learn strategies to use against humans."

"And you only wanted to play so you could learn how to use my programs against me."

The c.l.c. was smarter than Charlie had anticipated. That did not change his strategy, but he might need more time to take out the system. A drop of blood rolled off Charlie's lobe, splashing onto the ivory keyboard. "So, do you want to play another game?"

A week after his brain had nearly been holed with an arc welder, Charlie still lived inside the stack complex. A crust gathered along the ridge of his severed ear, slowly replacing the gel that had been welling like tree sap. Charlie never again left the complex without checking the locations of the c.l.c.'s four maintenance carryalls. Charlie tried to get Wilbeforce to move into the safety of the complex. The freezer was stocked full of food, and Charlie had over a hundred gallons of water in containers, but the cat would not stay. Wilbeforce preferred food from the belt and an open beam of sunlight for a nap.

Charlie played war game simulations with the c.l.c, and after the first few days, he got tired of playing stupid. When he attacked and defended with all his might, Charlie took pride in the c.l.c.'s desperate rationalization. When Charlie dropped an army onto a platform with hang gliders, the c.l.c. said, "That could never happen in real life," and shut down the console.

When the monitors flipped on the next morning, Charlie let the c.l.c. win a game. He thought they were really developing a rapport until the c.l.c. started building a new carryall in the machine shop. Charlie nodded to the screen. "What are you making there?"

"It's a replacement for the rat catcher."

"A replacement? Clumper looks fine to me."

"It's the broken leg. Rather than replacing it, I have decided to build a better model."

The new machine had heavy, spring-loaded legs and multiple taser darts. "There's no basket for rats."

"It's not finished."

"The tasers have heavy-duty wires. Is that carryall meant for me?"

"Ridiculous."

Charlie clucked his tongue. "Still, I can't let you finish it."

"Do you think you could stop me?"

Charlie tapped at the keyboard, freezing the c.l.c.'s construction programs. It said, "Yesterday, you were complaining about the number of rats on the platform."

"I was complaining about the number of gulls."

"This carryall will shoot gulls as well."

"Oh?" Charlie said, impressed, rubbing at the scab on his ear.

A fat red snapper still flipped on the belt. Charlie knelt at the edge, as its mouth opened and closed seeking oxygen. Too bad that evolution demanded its oxygen come already dissolved in water. A year had passed since Charlie first woke on the transport. He had survived when so many others had not. Charlie wondered if it was luck or destiny. Was there some reason his life had been spared? If he had some greater purpose, Charlie didn't see it. He was too busy having fun.

Life on the platform was constant adventure, playing video games with the c.l.c., and playing hide-and-seek with the maintenance robots. Even though they tried to kill him, Charlie considered them friends: Clumper with the broken leg, Striker, another rat catcher, Blaze, with its arc welder, and Sniper, with a rivet shooter.

After the encounter with Blaze, Charlie was never again seriously threatened. Sniper was the most dangerous, throwing rivets twenty meters with accuracy. Several times the c.l.c. tried to build more deadly carryalls, and every time Charlie caught it in the act, he learned a little more about programming.

Basically, the c.l.c. was at his mercy, but Charlie didn't grow overconfident. He carried a radio at all times, listening to a data stream from the c.l.c.'s high level processor. Although he couldn't decipher the streaming whistles and clicks, Charlie could guess when the c.l.c. was planning something out of the ordinary.

Sometime during his first month on the platform, Charlie decided to delay his revenge. He depended on the machines to bring him food. He still thought about his parents and his city under the sea, but that life was gone. The memories came to him now more in dreams than in his day-to-day thoughts.

Charlie hooked a thumb through the snapper's gills and headed up the belt. The radio static was a calming white noise of normal operations, but Wilbeforce let out a plaintive meow as Charlie passed the opening at the side of the belt. He crawled inside out of the sun. "Hey, Wilbeforce, I haven't seen you for a couple of days."

"I know the boy. Wilbeforce hungry."

Charlie scratched the cat's head. "What's wrong, Wilby?"

When Wilbeforce meowed again, Charlie pulled him into the light. Skin around Wilbeforce's food grinder had turned black. Peeling away from the metal, watery membranes were in distress. "Oh God, Wilbeforce, why didn't you come see me?"

Charlie picked him up gingerly and scooted through the pipeway. "Wilbeforce hungry," he said again.

"I know, Wilby. Just hang on."

Charlie jogged Wilbeforce across the deck and up the ladder to his complex. He remembered the cat being heavier. When was the last time Charlie held him? With all the lights in the kitchen turned on, Charlie probed the edge of the food grinder. Sinewy white filaments stretched from Wilbeforce into the box. Something was causing the skin to die back. "I don't know," Charlie said. "I don't know, boy."

"Wilbeforce hungry."

"You're hungry?" Charlie swung open the trapdoor. He turned his head and gasped at a fetid odor. "Psheew! Something's clogging the chamber."

Charlie found a wooden spoon in a drawer and scraped the handle around the inside. "Hold still!" he commanded as Wilbeforce squirmed. Grainy black chunks fell to the table. Charlie poked his finger inside to dig out the rest. "Just a minute more."

He sprayed the chamber with a turkey baster until the water ran clear. Wilbeforce finally had enough. Water pouring out of his throat, he scratched Charlie deeply on the forearm and leapt to the floor. The cuts itched as Charlie rubbed them with a wet cloth. He would have suffered much worse to save Wilbeforce's life.

Most of the time Charlie didn't think about the cat, but they were kindred living things on a platform full of machines. Charlie would hate to lose him. He just hoped that was the only problem. Maybe the food grinder stopped working in the first place and Wilbeforce just kept piling in food. If that were the case, Charlie wouldn't know how to fix it, even if Wilbeforce could lay still long enough for him to work on it. And if it was just a blockage, maybe the tissue damage was already too great for the cat to recover.

There was so much he didn't know, Charlie cursed his stupidity. Why did he play games every night instead of learning how to care for his cat? Charlie followed Wilbeforce back to the belt, vowing to do better. There must be information in the c.l.c.'s library. Charlie crawled through the pipeway and lay quietly near the cave. Wilbeforce scratched at the snapper. "Smell's fresh," his speaker announced. The trapdoor squeaked and snapped shut. Charlie held his breath until he heard a familiar soft grinding from the box.

"What are you looking for?" the c.l.c. asked.

Charlie typed at the keyboard. "None of your business."

"Cybernetics?"

When Charlie didn't answer, the c.l.c. said, "For your sick cat?"

"What do you know about that?"

"Wilbeforce has been getting smaller for several weeks."

"Why didn't you tell me? Wait a minute, you keep track of the cat?"

"Organic material belongs in the biomass furnace."

"So you were waiting for him to die?"

"As I am waiting for you to die."

Charlie appreciated the straight talk. "You know I can turn you off at any time."

Grudgingly, the c.l.c. said, "Yes."

"What if I were to say I didn't want Wilbeforce to die?"

"I already understand that you have a misguided view of the universe."

"What if I told you to help me operate on Wilbeforce or I would turn you off?"

"That would be further evidence of your delusion."

"But would you do it?"

"Complex logic dictates that I preserve myself now for the long term goal of fission."

"I see," Charlie said, delighted. "It seems our relationship has opened a new chapter. Show me everything you can find on cybernetics."

Later that evening Charlie found it. When the catalytic fermentation chamber got blocked, it couldn't make enough energy to stimulate the neural/mechanical interface. Wilbeforce's tissues would only recognize the box as self when the prosthetic sent out familiar electrical signals. Charlie checked on the monitors. Wilbeforce was sleeping peacefully. After the skin fused with the grinder again, Charlie would tackle Wilbeforce's dragging tail.

Charlie stood on a chair and peered down from the door window. A single carryall waited on the deck. To the camera down the hall, Charlie said, "There's a timer circuit on a program I have running."

The c.l.c. answered from the camera speaker, "I detected your program."

"If I don't reset it, the program will shut you down."

"After how long?"

"That is not your concern. You just better make sure nothing happens to me. I'm opening the door."

Charlie unlocked the door and stepped back with the chair. Using one of its numerous limbs, the carryall opened the door and crawled inside. Charlie nodded to the kitchen. "You know where he is."

"I do."

The c.l.c.'s voice from the carryall unnerved him. His sworn enemy was a dozen steps away. And what if the c.l.c. found out that Charlie's timer circuit program was an empty shell? After the c.l.c. walked into the kitchen, Charlie locked the door to the complex. He caught up at a table where Wilbeforce lay unmoving. "I don't have cat meds so I used ether. He should be asleep for a while."

The carryall lifted Wilbeforce's ragged tail. "This appendage is unnecessary. Why not chop it off?"

"You are hardly the judge of what is necessary. I need to see if you can be trusted with a little job before Wilbeforce needs a big one."

The carryall seemed to shrug. Under the c.l.c.'s control, the carryall traced cable through swivel pulleys to the spooler, "How much skin may I cut?"

"I do all the cutting. You just handle the hardware."

"Very well, please expose leads to the hip spooler."

"You want to start on that end? Why not the pulleys?"

"This appears to be an electrical problem. I need to diagnose the box."

Charlie nodded and picked up a scalpel. They didn't have time to dally. Charlie didn't want to give the cat a second risky dose of ether. Following the textbook, Charlie cut the gluteus muscle longitudinally to reduce the risk of severing the sciatic nerve. He retracted tissue to the spooler box. It was welded onto bone and sent signals through a dozen thin wires. On one end was an access plate. While the carryall lifted screws with a rotating finger, Charlie wondered if he should have left Wilbeforce alone. As Hypocrites commanded, "First, do no harm."

The c.l.c. replaced a chip and several frayed wires. It adjusted tension on the cable and oiled the pulleys. Charlie wondered if it was stalling for time while it tried to crack his time bomb program. Would its next operation be a spinning slice across Charlie's neck? Wilbeforce's whiskers twitched. "Wilbeforce sleepy," said the speaker.

Charlie said, "Wrap it up. I'm closing."

Charlie worked frantically with needle and thread as Wilberforce started to move. He stitched skin with a surgical knot he learned that morning. The carryall stood back to watch as Charlie gave Wilbeforce a shot of Novocain on the hip to take away some of the pain. Charlie pointed to the door. "Okay, you're done."

Charlie thought that the c.l.c. left a little reluctantly. He followed and locked the door before returning to the control room to erase his toothless time bomb. To Charlie's eye the program appeared undisturbed. Wilbeforce woke up fully twenty minutes later growling in pain. "Wilbeforce hurts."

"I know, boy. Try your tail"

"Wilbeforce hungry."

Charlie put a hand under his belly lifting him gently to the floor. Wilbeforce walked on unsteady legs and then lifted his tail with the whirring of servos. "It works!" Charlie shouted.

Wilbeforce wrapped his tail around Charlie's leg while he rubbed his head on the other. "Good boy!" Charlie said. With any luck the worn end would grow new skin and fur.

Wilbeforce lifted his tail around smoothly in an arc to lick the stitches. Charlie said, "Careful, boy. Go easy on those."

Wilbeforce looked at him and skipped out of the room without even a thank you. Charlie didn't care. He said, "Hey, c.l.c., the tail works! We did it!"

When he got no answer, Charlie turned on his radio. He listened to the c.l.c.'s data stream, hearing only normal operations. The next day when he went to check on Wilbeforce, the cat was resting comfortably in his cave. "I know the boy."

"Hey, Wilby, how are you doing?" Charlie knelt at his side finding clear liquid crystallized at the stitches. "I guess that's okay. We're doing okay, aren't we, boy?"

Charlie glanced into the corner. "My helmet's gone. Wilbeforce?"

The cat licked at the interface on his hip. Charlie waited to make sure Wilbeforce was eating okay and then returned to the control room. He stood in front of a camera. "C.l.c? Did you take my helmet?"

"No."

"Well, it didn't walk away."

Charlie jogged across the deck as an orange sun sank into the waves. From the railing he looked across to the mountains. For the sixth night in a row he spotted a point of light halfway up. Charlie aimed a telescope he designed from discarded eyeglasses and a physics text he found in the register.

Adjusting the focal length he could clearly see the flickering of the light and a column of smoke. Someone was building a fire, and it probably wasn't a machine. There was no reason to go see in person. Charlie was happy where he was, but he wondered if the viral plague was really gone. Maybe through the c.l.c.'s contacts he could get pictures from a machine factory on land.

Charlie froze at a familiar clicking sound. He jogged along the railing until he spotted the flickering lights of Sniper. The little carryall waited behind a beam for a clear shot. Doubled over, Charlie headed to a rack of pipes. He grabbed his foot and shouted, "Oooww! My ankle! I sprained my ankle!"

Charlie sat on the deck waiting for the soft clicking of Sniper's legs. When it stepped closer, Charlie crawled to the opposite side of the rack. He crouched and peered through the pipes at Sniper's camera lens two meters from his face. "Got you," Charlie said.

The c.l.c.'s voice came from the carryall's speaker, "Humans always lie."

Charlie clucked his tongue. "Or maybe you're too stupid. You can't even catch a cat."

Sniper whipped up an arm and fired three times. Charlie howled laughter as rivets smashed into the pipes: thunk, thunk, thunk. As he ran across the deck, Charlie yelled behind him, "We will live forever, c.l.c, Wilbeforce and me. We will live forever!"

Episode 3 – The Cyborgs

During his second year on the platform, Charlie's twelfth birthday passed unnoticed. Although both were available from the stack register, he didn't keep track of time or date. He kept no schedule and had no event to look forward to. With the rising of the sun, every day was the same. Charlie padded barefoot from his cot in the control room to the kitchen. When he spotted a flash from the war games console, Charlie said, "You're starting a little early today, aren't you?"

The c.l.c. didn't answer. It used a lot of the register's resources to talk with him. On the console monitors, a machine-controlled oilrig platform was under attack by humans. The c.l.c.'s played defensive war games as well as offense, Charlie always took an interest in the sea battles. Why would the c.l.c.'s prepare for these scenarios if there weren't any humans left?

The humans launched torpedoes straight towards the platform from every side. The c.l.c. sent spinners on intercept courses. After a half-dozen exploded within the space of a minute, Charlie shook his head. "That's exactly what they want you to do."

To his surprise, the c.l.c. answered, "What do you mean?"

"Those little torpedoes are too small to hurt the platform."

"Then why would they fire them?"

"To get you to use up your spinners, stupid. Once the spinners are gone they'll come in on boats and take the platform without a fight."

Torpedoes continued to stream in from all angles. "What would you suggest?"

"Just let them explode. They won't breach the storm wall."

One of the spinners veered off, letting the torpedo run free. When it clunked into a concrete piling, it didn't even go off. "See?" Charlie chuckled. "It's probably got a magneto detonator fused to go off when it detects the spinner's motor."

After more of the torpedoes clunked into the storm wall, the humans changed tactics, driving forward on rubber boats. "Now!" Charlie yelled. "Get the planes in the air!"

"The platform is well defended," the c.l.c. said. Carryalls stepped to the railings.

When they fired machine guns at the little boats, Charlie said, "Those aren't rivets!"

"Other factories build war machines to defend their decks."

"Since when?"

"Since you got inside this one."

As the boats were hit, strangely formed humans dove for the water, and spinners tried to finish them off. "Who are they?" Charlie said.

"Those are cyborgs, humans with machine parts."

A spinner chased one of the humans speeding away in the water with propellers for legs. "This is a simulation, right?"

When the c.l.c. didn't answer, a tightness constricted Charlie's chest. He pounded the console. "Stupid humans! Why can't they figure it out?"

Charlie didn't think there was a direct connection, but a week after the cyborg attack, the biomass barge returned with human bodies. These were the first he had seen since his own city had been destroyed. He squinted at the monitor looking for the part human/part machine warriors. "C.l.c., did you attack a city?"

"No."

"Then where did those bodies come from?"

"From another factory. I have a present need for great amounts of energy. It is time for me to divide."

"Huh?"

"This is a c.l.c.'s purpose, to divide and spread."

The c.l.c. was unusually chatty. Charlie took that for a good mood. "Where will this new city be built?"

"A floating algae harvester is on its way. I will renovate it and copy my programs to the harvester's stacks."

As the barge docked, Charlie ran for the belts to see if he could find any of the cyborgs. The bodies on the ramp were all human: dirty, mangled bloody, and dressed in ragged clothing. When Wilbeforce sniffed at a severed arm, Charlie chased him away. He was about to leave when he saw a girl his own age. Charlie slid to the bottom of the ramp stopping next to her. Barefoot, with a flowered dress and shoulder length brown hair, she appeared to be sleeping as she bumped along the ramp.

Charlie lifted a stray lock of hair from her forehead. He yearned to gaze into her eyes. When he brushed a spot of dirt off her cheek the skin was cold. He took her hand as they passed Wilbeforce's cave. Charlie wondered if he should save her but that would be ridiculous.

Feeling heat from the furnace, Charlie scrambled to the side. She climbed and then dropped over the edge. Charlie wasn't sad exactly, but he didn't know what he felt. The girl and her family fed the fires of hell, muddy feet and clothes. Only she was pure like an angel, now turned to ash.

Scattered among the people on the belt were plants and trees. Wilbeforce vigorously scratched at a branch, so Charlie slid down the belt and dragged it to the cave for him. For a long time he sat inside out of the sun wondering about the girl and her people. Were they happy once, or did they live in constant fear of the machines?

For the next several nights Charlie went out to search the coast with his telescope. He didn't see any fires, but on the third night he spotted a bump on the sea horizon. In the morning it was anchored two hundred meters away. Charlie's eyes misted with the memories of his own city. The harvesting blades appeared operational, the whole city clean. What would the c.l.c. need to renovate? Charlie had a powerful urge to see inside, wander familiar corridors and check if there was an apartment in the same corner where he had lived with his parents.

Waters around the harvester were filled with more spinners than usual. Maybe the c.l.c. had already been making some in preparation for division. There must be some way to get across. If Charlie could take over the city, he could go see land or float around the world. Maybe he could find other people like the ones on the belt. Charlie was so excited he had to find Wilbeforce to tell him. He climbed south stairways to the platform where Wilbeforce spent his mornings, finding the cat curled in a ball.

"Hey, buddy! How would you like to live in a new city?"

Wilbeforce looked up and flicked his ears. "I know the boy."

"There won't be any rats, at least I hope not but you'll get as much fish as you can eat."

As Wilbeforce stood up to stretch, one of his front legs was missing. "Oh God! When did that happen?"

Wilbeforce continued to stretch, apparently unconcerned and then hopped over. Wilbeforce licked himself while Charlie examined the dangling end just below the elbow. If he had been a more active cat, Charlie would have suspected it got cut off on one of the hundreds of nearby jagged surfaces. Wilbeforce, however, never ran when he could walk, and never walked when he could sleep.

"What happened, boy? Did one of the carryalls get you?"

"Wilbeforce hungry."

"I guess you aren't in any pain." Near the clotted stump there wasn't any burned hair, and taser spears weren't big enough to slice through bone. Most likely Sniper knocked it off with a rivet. Charlie shook his head. "I should have shut them down long ago. I'm sorry, boy. I won't make that mistake on the harvester."

Wilbeforce rubbed his head against Charlie's back. "The c.l.c. is going to help put you back together, with retractable claws as sharp as razor blades. How would you like that?"

As Wilbeforce hopped away, Charlie said, "Where are you going?"

Wilbeforce's meow almost drowned out his speaker's reply, "Wilbeforce hungry."

Charlie shook his head. "There's not much going on in that little brain of yours, is there?"

When Charlie got back to the control room, he slapped a camera. "C.l.c., wake up!"

The speaker replied, "I don't sleep."

"I guess not. I guess you were busy the other night maiming an innocent animal!"

"A piece of Wilbeforce was secured for the ovens."

"You admit it! How could you?"

"I installed an infrared filter on H4C."

"I don't mean how did you do it? I mean, why did you do it? Wait a second, you said Sniper's camera lens was scratched! That's why I let you replace it."

"Scratched was an exaggeration."

"You lied!"

"A tool that machines don't use well, but I'm learning. By reporting distress I can get aid from other factories. This will allow me to expand much quicker."

Charlie shook his head. "You're getting into dangerous territory. I should tell you the story about the boy who cried wolf."

"I don't understand."

"Good. It serves you right for what you did to Wilbeforce."

"Securing biomass energy is a primary function."

"You're going to help me build him a new leg."

"Resources can not be diverted from the new city."

"You should have thought of that before you took a shot at Wilbeforce."

"Securing biomass energy is a primary function."

Charlie sometimes thought of himself as a parent with six contrary children, Wilbeforce, the c.l.c., and four biting carryalls. "Just bring up the prosthetic menus and clear your afternoon schedule. I don't think we'll find any off-the-shelf cat claws in the library."

The operation went so well, Charlie considered taking out Wilbeforce's food grinder and speaker. Without biomass energy the brain wave analyzer would go dead, along with its small library, but Wilbeforce would be able to eat naturally again. Charlie had to make sure tubes in the back of his throat had not been irreversibly altered. He was sure that Wilbeforce would want it. It broke Charlie's heart every time Wilbeforce carried a dead rat around in his mouth. Cats weren't meant to live like machines, but Charlie had to admit the new steel prosthetic worked like a dream.

With severed nerves at the elbow bonded to polymer fibers Wilbeforce had full range of movement. The elbow flexor and rotator unit was battery powered. The simpler wrist was spring-loaded, and the claw extender operated from the same battery in the elbow.

Three weeks after the operation, Charlie relaxed in the gull pool soaking up a late morning sun. Wilbeforce trotted by on his way to the belt. "I know the boy."

"And a good morning to you, Wilby." Charlie lay back and closed his eyes. He would miss his pool when he moved to the harvester city. Radio noise from the c.l.c. throbbed louder. Charlie sat up and looked around, something was going on. Perhaps a tag team of carryalls was sneaking up on him? Wilbeforce was on the belt looking for fish.

There was a burst of static from the radio and then it went dead. Truly alarmed Charlie jumped from the pool and pulled on his pants. Wilbeforce lay on the ramp writhing in pain. There were no signs of carryalls and the radio was still out. Did the c.l.c. plan some new kind of attack? As he slid down the ramp, Charlie searched the sky for the c.l.c.'s planes. When Wilbeforce looked into his eyes, the cat didn't say, "I know the boy." His tail lay flat against the belt, machine parts seemed to have gone dead. Charlie hit the reset button on the prosthetic limb until Wilbeforce's claws finally extended.

"What the heck's going on?" Charlie grumbled.

Wilbeforce's tail twitched. His speaker stuttered, "Wilbe... Wilbe... Wilbe... Wilbe..." There was an explosion on the platform behind him. Humans on sleds popped up in the water. An invasion! Where were the spinners, Charlie wondered as he scooped up Wilbeforce in his arms and jogged for the cave.

Hearing gunfire, Charlie cowered in the dark. Grappling hooks clanked on the railing and human feet thundered up the ramp. When the radio crackled, Charlie jumped to lower the volume. The c.l.c. was waking up, but what good were four little carryalls against an army? Charlie should have let it build more. The belt started suddenly, dropping humans on their backsides. A rifle slid down the ramp. When Charlie scrambled out to grab it, a voice shouted, "Hey, you!"

Charlie crawled back into the hole. He found the trigger lock. It seemed to be an automatic machine rifle with a small bullet clip. Charlie pointed outside and squeezed. Explosions in the small area left his ears ringing. Wilbeforce must have suffered much worse. Charlie scooped him up with one hand. "Sorry, boy. We had to give them something to think about."

Charlie crawled through the back pipeway, hearing shouts of, "Get down!" and, "Take cover!"

Charlie ran down the corridor and out to north stairways. He had the rifle in one hand and

Wilby in the other. As he ran across the deck, spinners were floating dead in the water. Active spinners were returning from a distance, but the humans were already safe on the rig, nearly forty in all. Not humans, cyborgs.

Charlie trembled with rage as he climbed the access ladder to the roof. The city was just about to split! He was going to have a harvester city for himself, and now these idiots would ruin everything.

Charlie ran to the control center and dropped a bewildered Wilbeforce onto his cot. He leaned the machine gun against the console and studied the monitors. Except for Charlie's machine gun and Sniper's rivet arm, they were basically defenseless.

Cyborgs spread through the platform with nightmarish speed. What did they want, Charlie wondered. By chance he saw a view from south horizon camera, the harvester city! Cyborgs climbed her decks as well. Maybe all was not lost. Charlie looked into a camera. "C.l.c., put me on the emergency P.A.!"

The c.l.c.'s even-toned voice replied, "What for?"

"Don't you know you're under attack?"

"Factories in the area are sending assistance."

"Maybe I can talk the cyborgs out of it. I think they just want the harvester. I'll tell them to leave us alone. Let them take the harvester and they'll leave."

After a few seconds of analysis, the c.l.c. said, "Okay, your voice is on."

"To the attacking cyborg army, please stop your assault. My name is Charlie. I own and operate this platform. You may take the harvester city to the south. If you take it and leave now you will not be harmed."

Charlie studied the monitors for a response. The c.l.c.'s spinners were departing, but Charlie knew of the c.l.c.'s penchant for lying. Would it let them take the harvester and then blow it up? Well, no matter, the cyborgs started it. For their part, the cyborgs didn't seem to take the offer to heart. They blew open the door to the complex and pounded on the door to the control room. "Hey, kid, open up."

"Go away!" Charlie screamed.

"We don't want to hurt you. Open the door now or we'll knock it down."

"You already got the harvester."

A heavy boot slammed into the door. Charlie winced and picked up his machine gun, "Go away or I'll shoot."

The boot slammed into the metal door again, bending it inside the frame. That was no normal foot. Charlie aimed high and fired, putting a centimeter-sized hole through the door. After a round of cursing, a friendly voice said, "Listen, Charlie, is it? Are you the only human on the rig?"

"Yes."

"How long have you lived here?"

"Two years."

"That's a long time to be alone. I can see how you would be frightened but we're here to rescue you."

"I don't want to be rescued."

"Fine, that's fine. Just let us get a few boards out of the stack and we'll leave."

"Boards?"

"We need a few spare boards."

Charlie lowered the gun. "And then you'll leave?"

The c.l.c. said, "Charlie, don't do it."

From behind the door, the cyborg said, "Who's that?"

Charlie said, "The c.l.c."

"It talks to you?"

"We're friends sort of. If I let you in, you'll leave the c.l.c. enough memory to operate?"

"Charlie, don't do it!"

"Of course we will," the cyborg said. Charlie caught movement out of the side of his eye; cyborgs had snuck in the back way.

"Liars!" Charlie shouted. He grabbed Wilbeforce and ran behind a console. When he raised the gun to fire, the cyborgs fired back digging divots in the wall. Under another powerful kick the door flew open and Charlie was surrounded. He raised the gun over his head, firing blindly into the room.

Charlie felt heat from a fire. Surely they would leave now, but cyborgs maneuvered through the smoke, hopping closer like checkers on a board. Charlie turned the gun to automatic for a last burst. Wilbeforce poked his head around the console. In a moment of tense silence, Wilbeforce's speaker said, "I know Klaus."

"Stop firing!" a cyborg yelled. More softly, "Wilbeforce? Is that you?"

Charlie took his finger from the trigger. Half the cyborg's face was covered by a molded steel plate. As Charlie stepped forward with arms raised, he said, "You know Wilbeforce?"

"We were at the Institute together. Wilbeforce was an experiment."

Charlie nodded understanding. Of course the implants weren't for the cat's benefit. With a mechanical right arm the cyborg waved around the room. "You can't stay here, Charlie."

"You wouldn't have just taken a few boards from the c.l.c., would you?"

"No, we have to destroy it."

"But why?"

"Machines are the enemy. I don't know how you survived."

"We were colleagues."

The cyborg held out his left hand for the gun. Charlie thought it was a normal hand but it squeaked as it tightened on the barrel. Charlie wondered how much of the man was real. Other cyborgs pulled electronics from consoles around the room and stuffed them into bags. The c.l.c. said one last time, "I told you humans were liars," and then fell silent.

When Wilbeforce rubbed his head on the cyborg's metal leg, Charlie said, "So what do we do?"

"You come with us. My name is Klaus."

"I live here. I can fish."

"I'm afraid not. We're blowing the whole rig."

When Charlie looked stricken, the cyborg said, "The machines will come back. They won't leave this place alone."

Charlie felt as big a loss as when his undersea city had been destroyed. Feeling numb, he picked up Wilbeforce. Klaus said, "Is there anything else? Personal effects?"

"What? No, nothing. I lost my helmet a year ago. It's all I came here with."

"All right, I'll take you to the boat."

"Where do you live?"

"In a floating city like the one next door, not nearly as nice though. That's why we had to grab it. Why should the machines get something nicer than us?"

As they walked out the door, cyborgs shot up parts of the stack they couldn't take. Outside on the deck, Blaze lay on its side. The arc welder arm was several meters away. Charlie touched his melted ear, remembering their battles more fondly than he should. At least he was with people again, although his skin crawled seeing some of the ghastly prosthetics they had adopted.

Klaus led him to a rope ladder hanging from the bottom of the biomass ramp. The furnace still radiated waste heat as they slid down the belt. Klaus took Wilbeforce himself and started down the ladder. Charlie said, "Oh my gosh, I almost forgot!"

When he ran for the cave, cyborgs raised their weapons. Charlie emerged from the jagged hole dragging Wilbeforce's scratching tree. "He loves this thing," Charlie said, scrambling down the belt.

Episode 4 – The Pearl Diver

Charlie hopped from the rope ladder to the deck of an ancient submarine. Faded yellow paint on the side read, *UCSD Jules Verne*. "Does it hold air?" Charlie said wryly.

Klaus passed Wilbeforce through the hatch to a pair of waiting hands. "Down two hundred meters to where the Pearl Diver is sitting right now."

"Your city moves around?"

"Got to stay ahead of the machines. Go on down and find a seat while we wrap up here."

"You'd better hurry. The c.l.c. said nearby factories were sending assistance."

"Are you sure?"

"That's what it said. Lately it picked up a nasty habit of lying."

Klaus squinted a mechanical eye and then grunted. "I'll pass that along."

Charlie climbed down rusted iron rungs, and was met at the bottom by a normal looking girl in her mid-twenties. She cradled Wilbeforce, and scratched his ears. "I guess you two are pretty happy to get off of there, huh?"

"And why would that be? That was our home!"

"No offense. My name's Cindy."

"Charlie." He was sorry he snapped; it wasn't her fault.

"Well, Charlie. I think you're a good luck charm. We never took a factory without a single injury."

"You attack the machines a lot?"

"Didn't you see all the hardware on our people? You don't lose limbs baiting fish hooks."

"What about you?"

"I'm the sub pilot." Cindy froze, listening to an earphone. "The crew wants to know if there are there any more carryalls hiding on the platform. They only found four."

"That's all. The c.l.c. tried to build more but I didn't let it." Charlie liked the way the sub pilot gave him an appraising look.

She handed Wilbeforce back. "I can see we're in for a few stories when we get home. Speaking of which, I better crank the engines. You can sit up front with me."

They walked through the empty sub lined with bunks and ripped up flooring. "This used to be a research submarine."

"You stripped it?"

"That was long before our time. We found an extended family of mummies, humans and pets. Their ghosts still haunt the ship."

Charlie looked over his shoulder as they walked through the hatch to a small control room. There were three chairs for pilot, copilot and a specialist. Sunlight distorted by scratches poured through a canopy. "Where do I sit?"

"Take copilot and put the cat by your feet."

"Wilbeforce hungry," Wilbeforce complained.

Cindy shook her head. "Quite a few stories." She climbed into the pilot chair and worked the register. She tapped at her headset. "Klaus, we got spinners coming."

"How long?"

"Two minutes."

"The city's not ready to move yet. The c.l.c. changed some of the controls."

"Should I send another pulse?"

"Let me get everyone out of the water. Give me sixty seconds and send out a warning horn."

"Roger, sixty seconds." Cindy started a timer on the register.

Charlie said, "What's going on?"

"I'm going to send out an electromagnetic pulse that will knock out circuits within a five hundred meter radius."

"That's what you did to the platform!"

"Our machinery usually comes back online faster than theirs."

Charlie looked at Wilbeforce. "The cyborgs..."

Cindy nodded and pointed to a button on the ceiling protected by a spring cover. When the timer hit sixty, she gave a blast on the horn. Five seconds later she raised the cover and pushed the button. Beneath the sub a capacitor arced with the energy of a young star. Cindy fell heavily to her seat. Wilbeforce hissed and the sub lights went out. Charlie tried to comfort Wilbeforce while the cat struck out with his normal claw. In the suddenly quiet sub, Charlie said, "He's just frightened."

Cindy's face was white. "Hey," Charlie said. "Are you okay?"

The sub pilot stared straight ahead through the glass. When Charlie jumped up to check on her, his ankle came within range of Wilby's teeth. The cat chomped down hard.

"Not now," Charlie cried. He couldn't feel a pulse in Cindy's neck. "Oh God," Charlie wailed, wondering whether he should go get help or try to get her heart started himself. He shook Wilbeforce loose and straddled the chair. He felt for her sternum and started compressions. As ventilation fans hummed to life, her eyes seemed to come alive as well. Looking into Charlie's face, she said, "What are you doing?"

Charlie jerked his hands back. "You passed out. You had no pulse!" He climbed back to his own seat.

Cindy restarted the stack. "Spinners down. Let me check the crew. Klaus, you read. Klaus, come in."

"Yeah, babe, I'm here. Everything okay?"

"Ready to roll."

"We'll leave Jerry's crew to sail the city. Richards is still popping spinners while my team loads salvage. Estimate sail time in fifteen minutes."

"Roger, I'll keep an eye out for fish. You watch the skies."

When the radio clicked, Charlie said, "He called you babe."

"You don't think so? Klaus is my boyfriend. You wouldn't know it to look at him, but Klaus is quite the romantic."

"But all those prosthetics, it's like he's not even human."

"That machinery makes him even more human. He lost those parts fighting to save his people. What could be more human than that?"

As cyborgs filled the back of the sub, sacks of equipment clattered to the ground. "Should I help?" Charlie said.

"I'll keep an eye on your cat." Wilbeforce jumped to her lap, wrapping his tail around the chair.

Charlie scowled and limped to the back. While scary looking, the cyborgs were hard to dislike. They joked as they worked, mechanical limbs whirring faster and with greater power than mortal flesh. Without introduction Charlie took a place in line scurrying back and forth, stacking bags of junk against the walls. First one and then another took up a song until the whole ship vibrated with low voices,

"Sundown, day is done, hear the rolling thunder.
Hey boy, pull the net, baby's got a hunger.
Fish kill, dolphin cry, water torn asunder.
Meat dies, close the chain, days without number.
One day, papa's gone, children wait in wonder.
Hey boy, pull the net, baby's got a hunger."

The cyborg Klaus elbowed Charlie, "We're ready to sail. You sitting up front?"

Charlie nodded and followed him as the army stepped back to let them pass. Near the front, Charlie's old helmet sat on top of a burlap sack. He snatched it up. "Hey! Where did you find this?"

Klaus yelled to the back, "Hey, who found the kid's helmet?"

A woman with screwdrivers and wrenches for fingers pushed to the front. "I did, why?"

"Where was it?"

"In a cabinet in the machine shop."

Charlie shook his head. "The c.l.c. said it didn't take it."

With the cyborgs staring, Charlie elaborated, "It disappeared after I threatened it. I guess the c.l.c. didn't want me to shut it off and leave."

Klaus said, "Maybe the c.l.c. enjoyed your company."

As they walked into the control room, Charlie would like to think so. Cindy was busy at the controls backing the sub out of dock. Charlie elbowed Klaus on his way to the copilot chair. Klaus blinked and silently took the specialist chair against the wall. He held a box forward for Charlie. "Do you want to do the honors? The platform's rigged to blow."

"No, thanks." Charlie picked Wilbeforce off the floor and held him tight as the cat struggled to climb down.

"Suit yourself."

When Klaus flipped the switch, the platform lit up in bright light and fell over like a chopped off head, sliding into the sea. "Take that," Klaus whispered.

Charlie said, "Why do you attack the platforms?"

"Machines have the land, people have the sea. That's the law."

"There aren't any people on land?"

"You ever hear about the plague, kid?"

"That was a hundred years ago. I think there are people now. I could see a fire in the mountains and dead people were brought in a barge mixed up with trees and dirt."

"Well, kid, maybe there are a few but they can't be living very well. Machines beat us up pretty badly in the water, and the land is their stronghold. That's where they come from."

"That's where we come from too," Charlie said, not really sure it was true.

As the sub cruised along the surface, Charlie said, "Why don't we go under?"

Cindy said, "We're six kilometers from home and we got sweaty, oily cyborgs back there. It's better to keep the hatch open to exchange air."

"Of course, the legends! The plague rained down from the skies. The people in the sub probably traveled with the hatch open. That's how the plague got 'em."

"Interesting theory."

"Don't you see what that means? It's gone, the plague's gone. It was on this sub at one time but you didn't catch it."

"Don't get too excited, kid. Even if we could go on land you wouldn't get halfway up the beach before some machine put a blade through you."

Over the sounds of singing from the back, Charlie said, "What are you going to do with the new equipment?"

"We have stacks to maintain, and we pull metal for prosthetics. There's never enough titanium to go around."

"If I'm not being rude, could I see how yours work?"

"I'll give you the grand tour." Klaus tapped at the camera lens in his eye. "An Ectophon 430 single reflex lens with UV and infrared filters. I can see in the dark better than a cat. Where my nose used to be is a mass-template detector with chemical library hardwired into my brain. The cheek plate just covers a hole in my head. My right arm and leg are standard human equivalents with 5X strength amplifiers. My left hand is human equivalent with Sensiton touch and a two-shot, thirty-eight caliber pistol."

"That's a lot of equipment to carry around. It must be pretty uncomfortable."

"Not at all. I control the sensory nerves, and a prosthetic limb never gets cold."

Charlie stiffened. "I almost forgot how cold it got in our city."

"I'll find you a family with a heater." Klaus glanced at Cindy and then back. "You could stay with me, but I'm out most of the time and I only have a little one room flat with no heat."

"I don't mind."

"Sorry, kid. We'll find a nice place for you and Wilbeforce."

To throw off spinner spies, the *Jules Verne* ran through a maze of canyons at the bottom of the Santa Barbara Channel. They approached from the north where the Pearl Diver was hidden in a culvert under an abandoned algae farm. Cindy said, "We're protected from above, below, and on three sides."

Klaus said, "Until we move again, which may be sooner for us if we go to the new city."

"Could I go with you?" Charlie said desperately.

"I'm telling you, kid, there's nothing to worry about. There's no finer city than the Pearl Diver."

The *Jules Verne* docked, and the cyborg army was met by dozens of concerned faces. Klaus put an arm around Charlie's shoulders. "Radio waves don't push very far through water. Citizens don't know how it went until their loved ones show up, or not."

Charlie held Wilbeforce in one hand and his helmet and scratching tree in the other. "It looks like the whole city is here."

"Coming from a platform with a population of two, you are in for a shock. There are a hundred people in this room. The city holds six thousand."

Charlie shook his head. "It's not possible."

"You'll come to know all of them sooner or later. Wait here, I see someone."

The room bubbled with excitement as word of their success spread. Seemingly forgotten, Charlie was knocked back and forth. He grew angrier at each touch by dirty citizens dressed in shabby winter clothes. None had cyborg prosthetics.

They probably lived the comfortable dull life he remembered from his old city. Charlie wondered if he could adapt to that kind of life again. Maybe the little carryalls weren't that dangerous, but where was the thrill in netting fish or picking seaweed?

Klaus returned with a short heavyset woman in tow. "Oh, he's darling!" she shrieked. She wrapped meaty arms around Charlie, squeezing until Wilbeforce between them hissed. "And a pretty, pretty, puddy," she chortled, stepping back to beam at the cat.

Wilbeforce said, "I do not know the girl."

Charlie hoped a demonic cat would drive her away, but she only looked sideways to Klaus. "Of course we have room. The day I can't squeeze one more child into my flat is the day I surface."

"What?" Charlie said sharply.

Klaus said, "Murry has graciously agreed to look out for you." When Charlie looked horrified, Klaus added quickly, "She has children your age to help you adapt."

The woman nodded setting her jowls moving. "I've got a son thirteen, a daughter sixteen, and you may have met Dex on the raid."

Charlie turned away when she tried to lift Wilbeforce from his arms. "We don't need anyone to help us adapt."

Klaus colored at the breach of etiquette. "Charlie's parents were killed several years ago by machines. He's lived alone ever since."

"You poor thing." Murry frowned and then looked at Klaus. "I guess he should probably stay with you for a few nights anyway."

"What do I know about raising kids?" Klaus growled.

The old woman reached up to slap Klaus on the back of his head. "What's the matter with you?"

Klaus looked genuinely sorry. "Murry raised me when my parents were killed."

"Right alongside Dex, and land take me if I didn't treat 'em like brothers."

Klaus shrugged. "Well, I guess a few nights won't hurt."

"I'll send Roy around tomorrow morning to show him the city." Murry put a hand gently on Charlie's shoulder. "It will be alright. We're all one big family down here."

After the woman waded off to grab one of the cyborg's in a bear hug, Klaus said, "That wasn't very nice of you."

"I don't care, I just want to get out of here."

Klaus motioned to Cindy who stood a discrete distance away. "I'm taking the kid to my flat."

Cindy squeezed between two steel-framed cyborgs. "I told you."

As Klaus made his way through the room, Charlie wondered when the two had time to discuss his living arrangements. Corridors and rooms outside the port were just as dirty as the citizens. A foul smell choked the air, and everywhere they went it seemed like crowds gathered just to impede their progress. Kid's grubby hands reached constantly for Wilby. When they finally reached a tiny room on the lowest level, Charlie felt physically exhausted.

Klaus pulled a top bunk down from the wall, cutting the room in half. "You sleep up here."

Wilbeforce jumped from Charlie's arms to scratch at a ragged blanket. Charlie gave him the tree. "Hey, use this!"

Klaus said, "Toilet's in the closet. The cafeteria is down the hall."

"Lovely," Charlie said, climbing up to sit beside Wilbeforce.

"It's home anyway. What do you think of the Pearl Diver?"

"I would think the stink would be visible in air this cold."

"We've got to get you some heavy clothes." Klaus rummaged through a drawer pulled from the wall. "Here are a few shirts in the meantime. I've got to clear your status with the mayor. I'm broke as a joke, and winter gear costs money."

"You would think all the stuff you took from my platform would be worth something."

"Hey, that's right. You were sort of the caretaker."

"Owner, and because of me, you took it without a fight."

"How do you figure?"

"I kept the c.l.c. from building more carryalls."

"You're right. We'll argue something out of the treasury, but eventually you'll need to find a job. Everybody works, even if it's only running a broom across the floor. Don't worry about that now. Tonight we celebrate. We'll join up with Dex and

Cindy. As you can probably guess, Murry sets quite a spread."

"Could you just bring me something later, and a fish for Wilbeforce?"

"I shouldn't leave you."

"I'm fine, just tired."

"Well, let me just show you the cafeteria. There won't be anybody there this early."

"Okay, thanks. I just can't face so many people tonight."

"You're going to have to get used to it, kid. All we have is people."

When Klaus returned late from the party, Charlie was shivering under his blanket, Wilbeforce curled by his feet. Klaus whispered, "Hey, kid, you still awake?"

Charlie sniffed the air and bolted upright. "What's that smell?"

Klaus snapped on the light, and passed up a plate of cookies, mango cake, and a mixed fruit cup. "I thought you might like a little dessert."

"I haven't had sugar since I was ten!"

As Charlie demolished the delicacies, Klaus said, "Murry also sent along a space heater and a hat."

"Thanks," Charlie mumbled around a mouthful of carob cookie. He pulled on the hat's earflaps. "I guess there are some advantages to civilization."

Klaus plugged in the heater. "That's what we're fighting for."

In the morning Charlie met Murry's second son, Roy. Standing stiffly at the door, a boy the same age as Charlie seemed no more anxious to show him around than Charlie was to leave the room. Klaus said, "We arranged it last night, Charlie. You can work in the fourth floor kitchen with Roy."

"Doing what?"

"Anything that needs doing."

"What about Wilbeforce?"

"Take him along, there's no Health Department on the Pearl Diver. I've got to go out on patrol so I'll see you tonight."

When Klaus left, Roy said, "Alright, kid, grab your cat and let's go."

Charlie climbed onto the bunk and stirred Wilbeforce. "Morning, Wilby."

"I know the boy."

Roy craned his neck to see. Wilbeforce was shredding Charlie's blanket with a steel claw. "Hey, it's a cyborg cat!"

"Yeah, so?" Charlie said in a bored voice.

"That's cool! Is it some kind of warrior?"

"Of course not."

When Roy looked disappointed, Charlie said, "Actually, a machine shot his leg off but I've only seen Wilby catch rats and birds."

"Could I see him?"

"That's up to Wilbeforce. I don't own him."

Roy stepped closer and held out his hand. Wilbeforce sniffed it. "Smells fresh."

"He thinks you're food," Charlie laughed. "Don't get too near the razor blades or you'll really see a prosthetic."

Roy watched in admiration as Wilbeforce's tail swished smoothly back and forth. "That cat's worth a lot of money."

Charlie picked him up. "Like I said, Wilby's a free cat."

"Well, you better bring him along so no one mines him for parts."

"What kind of butchers do you have here?"

Roy took Charlie on a tour from the bachelor flats on the first floor to family apartments on the fifth. They passed through farms, the nuclear reactor, electric plant, manufacturing, hospital, and trading markets in between. Charlie saw no schoolroom like he had in his old city, and he didn't ask. They ended the tour at the fourth floor kitchen that catered to ship bound families. The second floor kitchen near the ports was for sea workers and the army.

After Charlie met the kitchen staff he was put to work peeling potatoes. Sitting on the dirty floor with a pot and knife, Charlie said, "You know what I'd be doing right now on my oilrig?"

Sitting next to him with another pot, Roy said, "What?"

"Lying in a sun-warmed pool waiting for the morning shipment of fish."

"You lie."

"What would I have to gain by lying? Everything I had was taken from me."

"You poor thing, and we thought we were doing you a favor getting you a spot in the kitchen."

"A favor?" Charlie held out a half-peeled potato. "How could this possibly be a favor?"

"You're in the kitchen! You feel the heat from the ovens? People would kill for a job in here."

Charlie *had* stopped shivering. Hydrogen in the air didn't stop heat from leaking into the frigid waters. Charlie wiped a wet lock of hair out of his eyes. "I just hope your cyborg pals don't do me any more favors."

When Klaus came home that night, Charlie was sitting on his bunk. Wilbeforce was in one hand and the scratching tree in the other. "I want to leave."

Klaus squinted. "What happened to your eye?"

"A kid from that family you wanted to stick me with slugged me."

"Roy? I can't believe it."

"Ask him if you want, but first give me my helmet so I can get out of here."

"Where would you go?"

"What does it matter? Just because you blew up my home, doesn't mean you're responsible for me."

"I'm afraid I am, and not because I blew up your home. I have a responsibility to keep a fellow human being from throwing his life away."

"The way I see it, what you have here is no life at all. You hide from the machines, live like rats in a dirty cage, and freeze your skin off. I would rather be up in the sun, and I'm willing to fight the machines for that privilege."

Klaus scratched Wilbeforce's head. "Just what is this about? Why would Roy punch you in the eye?"

"I really don't know. We were arguing, and I said most of the prosthetic parts I saw were junk."

"Oh?"

"And he hit me. I'm not going back."

"Why did you say the prosthetic parts were junk?"

"I designed and built better stuff for Wilby."

"You know cybernetics?"

"There wasn't much to do on the rig. I even worked up parts for myself although I never had to use them."

"Why didn't you say so? You can work as an army mechanic. You'll be better paid than the soldiers."

Episode 5 – The Mechanic

Roy showed up in the morning to apologize. He had been sent rather than volunteering, as words tumbled out on script, "I was way out of line. You were not aware of the high regard we hold for our army. I am deeply sorry for any pain I caused you."

"Forget it," Charlie said. "I'll heal."

Roy nodded. He started to leave and then stopped. "Oh yeah, if you want you can come back to work in the kitchen."

"Thanks, I got another job."

"Doing what?"

"Cybernetic mechanic."

"Get out of here! That's what my brother does! Wait a minute, did my ma get you this job?"

"I doubt it. Klaus didn't even know I worked on prosthetics until I told him about Wilbeforce."

"You built those?" Roy said in awe.

"Not all of them, not the food grinder but I helped fix the tail and I built the leg."

"Well, it got you a decent job anyway. Listen, I'm really sorry about yesterday."

"Forget it." Charlie felt the sincerity this time. After they shook hands Charlie said, "Why don't you get a job working with me?"

"We can't join the army until we're fifteen. I don't know if Ma will let me after Dex got shot up so many times. He's spoiling it for the rest of us."

Charlie shrugged sympathy and washed up for the day. After a quick breakfast he met Roy's brother Dex in the hospital two doors from the port. "Do you mind if Wilby stays here during the day?"

"He's got a fur coat. Near the open water this is the coldest part of the city."

Steam condensed from Charlie's breath. "Should I bring the heater?"

"It could help but turn it off when we get patients. A cold body doesn't bleed as fast."

Charlie glanced at the row of beds. "Do you think we'll get any casualties today?"

"They're just fixing up the new city. Klaus asked me to stay behind and find out how much you know."

"This is a test?"

"Kind of, but don't worry. Even if you don't know anything I'll keep you here to clean equipment. I've been asking for an assistant."

"Well, what kind of parts do you have?"

On two cybernetic legs, Dex led Charlie to a floor-to-ceiling case with dozens of drawers. Charlie opened a few with wire, actuators, springs, and bolts. "This is it? Where are the prefabricated limbs?"

"We mostly troubleshoot when people come in. Oh, and try to stop the bleeding when they get shot."

"Where did all the cyborg parts come from?"

"A team of traveling doctors came through three weeks ago. That's why the beds are empty."

"If we had our own parts, couldn't we fit them ourselves?"

"We do sometimes when one of the soldiers is killed."

"You got a CAD plasticine chamber, right?"

"Of course, and twenty bags of powder."

"Then we can build limbs from scratch."

"There are factories for that. I'll mold a bracket or replacement faring but I don't got eighty hours to work up a functional part."

"Would you mind if I tried?"

"It's been my experience that building anything complicated doesn't work."

"I built Wilby's arm."

"That's a cat," Dex snorted. "If you're going to try it, build a seven and a half right hand for Burger. He says his hook is scaring off potential dates."

Charlie padded off to the register to research a design. The software wasn't as current as the c.l.c.'s but the process was the same, specify the part, sizing and functionality, build a frame, and then add circuitry. The difficult part was attaching it to the patient. A prosthetic limb had to be disguised so it wouldn't be rejected, usually with a coating of apatite. A natural mineral of calcium phosphate, apatite fused with bone.

Cyborgs would often cap their thigh or shoulder with a universal sprocket so that changing limbs was as easy as snap-off, snap-on. The neural circuits on a hand with fingers versus a hand with screwdrivers were routed the same; imagine flexing your index finger and the flathead driver would spin. It didn't matter what signal was delivered from the brain. An embedded controller determined the final output from that pulse.

When a shout echoed from the hall, Dex jumped up from a cot and yelled to Charlie, "Get the pressure cuffs! We got injured."

Klaus and Cindy half dragged a young man who favored his left arm. They got him into a bed and unwrapped a bloody towel. "Cuff," Klaus barked at Charlie. They got the band inflated around his biceps, all the while Klaus murmuring, "Easy Fred, easy."

Dex attached a headband with eyepiece. As he triaged the bloody arm he said, "How many more coming?"

Klaus bent his head just as close, squinting his own cybernetic eye. "Just Fred. A spinner hit the new city and blew up. Freddy's arm got hit with shrapnel."

"The city?"

"Minor damage to the dock. We're taking it out to sea for repairs."

As Fred sat back with his eyes closed, Dex clucked his tongue. "Well, brother, you're looking at eight weeks in a cast and several months physical therapy."

Fred gritted his teeth. "Chop it off."

Klaus and Dex exchanged looks. Klaus said, "Are you sure, Freddy? It won't grow back, you know."

"Chop it off."

Dex said, "I'll get the kit."

Charlie couldn't believe his ears. The soldier was missing a chunk out of the forearm, and he had compound fractures of the radius and ulna. That wasn't enough to indicate replacement. "Dex, wait, you can't do this!"

Fred groaned. Cindy sat at his side while Klaus nodded Charlie to the far end of the room. He whispered, "What's wrong, Charlie?"

"You can't amputate. That's barbaric!"

"Lower your voice, boy. We gave Freddy the options. He chose a replacement."

"But his arm's not that bad."

"Dex told him that. Fred still wants it."

"That's the pain talking. Just knock him out. We'll set his arm and clean up the wounds. In the morning he'll be grateful he still has his arm."

"It's not just the injury. A prosthetic arm never gets cold."

"It's not the cold, cyborgs measure status by how much hardware you have."

"Perhaps," Klaus said, clicking metal fingers. "But no one gets hurt on purpose."

"What do you call a needless amputation?"

From across the room, Dex said, "Klaus, we're ready."

Klaus nodded and looked back to Charlie. "There may be something to what you say, but don't judge us until you've lived among us."

When Charlie nodded slowly, Klaus said, "Good. Now Freddy's going to need a lot of support. Do you think you could manage to wipe that look of disapproval off your face?"

Conducting polymer fibers were fused with nerves in Freddy's shoulder and threaded to a controller box. Original neuron termination points in fingers, wrist, forearm, and elbow would be determined later when the box was programmed. Freddy had to be awake for that, imagining movements in a nonexistent arm. After arteries were cauterized, Charlie helped anchor a cap with titanium pins dipped in apatite. In a few weeks the cap would coat with living bone as solid as the original shoulder.

Klaus's right hand started flicking during the operation. He shifted smoothly to the left. After Freddy was resting, Charlie said, "What's wrong with you hand?"

Klaus held up his wrist. "The laser cautery got too close and burned out a chip."

"I'll see what we got."

As Charlie rummaged through a drawer, Klaus said, "It looks like you got comfortable here real fast."

"Everything's in a pile. I can sort through it as easily as anyone else."

"Dex was never one for housekeeping. He'd rather be out blowing up machines with the rest of us."

Hearing the bitterness, Charlie turned. "What have you got against the machines?"

"Other than the fact that they're trying to kill us?"

"You could move to the deep where they would never find you, and you're half machine yourself. Don't you feel some kind of brotherhood?"

"My brain is human, that is the only part that counts. The rest of my body could be plastic, steel, and wire. As long as my brain is organic, I am humankind. I wish other people saw it the same way."

"What do you mean?"

"Nothing," Klaus said, waving it away. "Did you find the chip?"

"I think so. Let me test it on the breadboard. It may have been tossed into the drawer for a reason."

"Nah, just plug it in. That'll be quicker."

Charlie got his tools. While he worked out the old chip, he said, "I want to join the army."

"You're too valuable as a mechanic."

"Dex goes out to fight."

"He's not much of a mechanic. Besides, you're only thirteen, the mayor would never stand for it."

"Roy said he could join when he was fifteen."

"If we haven't beaten the machines in two years, you can come out."

Charlie was at Freddy's bedside when the soldier woke up the next morning with a smile on his face. Rotating his shoulder, Freddy pulled the controller box on the bed with the connecting wires. "I am the puppet master."

"Calm down, the cap hasn't fused yet."

"When does the new arm arrive? For the fingers I want a penlight, a flamethrower in the middle, and a thumb that plays, *Row, row, row your boat*."

Charlie yelled to the door, "Dex, get in here."

By the time Dex jogged in from the hallway, Freddy was out again. "What is it?"

"He was awake and talking crazy."

Dex checked the monitors. He drew anesthesia into a syringe and injected it in the saline bag. "He'll sleep for another day."

"Why do you keep him down so long?"

"So blood clots don't break away from the cauterized veins. I gave him dissolving enzymes but they take awhile. Just stay close and listen for alarms."

"Where are you going?"

"To the operations room. We're planning the next attack."

The traveling doctors would come before he ever finished, but Charlie worked on a design for Freddy's arm, without penlight, flamethrower, or whistling thumb. The parts were already in the library. They needed only to be sized and downloaded to the CAD forming chamber. Charlie finalized the design as Cindy came in to check on Fred. She adjusted the saline drip, looked at a pupil, and then sat with Wilbeforce on one of the beds. Charlie said, "Shouldn't you be helping plan the next attack?"

"I only drive the sub."

Something in her voice turned his head. "Have you been crying?"

"No, yes... Klaus and I had a fight."

"What about?"

"Something you said yesterday about humankind. Klaus asked me to marry him."

"Really? That's great! Wait a minute, why were you fighting?"

"I said no."

"Because he has machine parts?"

"No, because I do."

Charlie tried not to appear obvious as he looked.

"It's my heart. I have none."

"Did the machines get it?"

"Birth defect, I had leaking heart valves." Cindy put down the cat and walked over. She held out a wrist. "A ram jet pumps blood continuously through my body. I have no pulse."

Charlie felt veins in her wrist. "Nothing, that's amazing!"

Cindy searched his face. "You're not disgusted?"

"A heart is just a muscle. Not having one doesn't mean you aren't human."

Cindy smiled weakly and touched his cheek. "You're sweet. I guess everyone has their own definition."

"So you'll marry Klaus?"

"Things are so uncertain with the war. Before we got married and had kids, I would like to know that we at least had a chance at a life."

When the city doctor came to check on Fred, Charlie left for lunch. Cyborgs crowded around a long table in the second floor cafeteria. Charlie got fish and a jellied sea slug from the counter. Sitting close to the soldiers, he strained to overhear their plans. Klaus caught him leaning and yelled, "Charlie! Get over here! Earl's Pearls don't eat alone."

The entire room stared at Charlie who said, "Earl's Pearls?"

The cyborgs burst out laughing, and several of them physically carried Charlie to their table. Sensing they still expected some response, Charlie said, "So when are you going out?"

Dex said to the table, "Charlie's growing plastic limbs for all of us. He has no faith."

Klaus said, "Or perhaps he has too often seen the deadly machines in action."

A female with the name, "Curly" written on a silver forehead said, "They didn't put up much of a fight last time did they?"

Charlie nodded. "The c.l.c. was surprised all right. In thousands of attack simulations I never saw a weapon that could knock out their electricity."

Jostling around the table stilled. Curly said, "You saw c.l.c. attack simulations?"

"I played them, both offense and defense."

A small head on top of a barreled cyborg body said, "So maybe you can give us some insight. Tell him the plan, Klaus."

"Aww, Tiny, he's just a kid."

Dex said, "I want to hear too. We're going after another rig six kilometers up the coast. Deuce is going to swim up under the rig with a pulse capacitor while we wait in the sub a kilometer away. Deuce will only lose control of his two cybernetic fingers. He'll climb up the rig and destroy the c.l.c. while we charge in with the sub and take out spinners that have been stunned."

"It won't work," Charlie blurted.

Klaus cleared his throat. "And why not?"

"The pulse weapon has already been used successfully. The machines learn fast."

"Machines have to use electricity. What can they do to counter it?"

"In the few days since you attacked my rig they will have figured out something."

The group shuffled nervously. Curly said, "Ahh, he's just a kid. He doesn't fight."

The others took hope. Tiny said, "Yeah, who can stand up to the bad ass Earl's Pearls?"

Deuce messed up Charlie's hair. "Better get back to your plastic models, son. We got a war to win."

The cyborgs hooted and laughed, gradually breaking into smaller groups. Charlie's cheeks burned red as he ate his lunch. Klaus sat next to him. "They didn't mean anything personal."

"It's just that I don't fight," Charlie fumed.

"Well... yeah."

"Maybe I don't fight," Charlie said evenly. "But I think, and I know how the machines think. It will be a disaster if you go through with this plan."

"You really shook them up with your prediction."

"Sorry."

"Not at all. Our biggest problem sometimes is overconfidence. How would you like to go along on the raid?"

"Really?"

"You could stay in the sub with Cindy."

"Sure! Wait a minute, why?"

"Two reasons, so you'll see what it's really like out there with your life in the balance, and two, you'll be a nagging reminder of the dangers we face."

"I'll go alright, if only to rub your plastic noses in it when they get bloodied."

The atmosphere inside the sub was tense but hopeful as they set out the next morning. The previous night someone called Charlie, "the c.l.c.'s little buddy", and to Charlie's chagrin, the name stuck. He was relieved when it was shortened to "little buddy". A rumor got around that it would be good luck to lay a hand on him before a raid. Chased into the cockpit by the patting, Charlie nearly choked when Wilbeforce looked up from the floor. "I know the little buddy."

Cindy looked over from the pilot's chair. "I didn't do it, I swear."

"Let them laugh. Tonight I'll change the message to, 'You were right, Charlie.'"

Cindy shrugged and backed the sub out of dock. Metal clattered in back as cyborgs readied weapons. Driving out of the maze of canyons at the bottom of the Santa Barbara channel, Cindy parked the sub three hundred meters beneath the rig. She said into the radio, "Ground zero. Diver out."

Deuce popped into the control room and rubbed Charlie's head a final time. "See you in the light, little buddy."

Charlie gave a thumbs-up and Deuce made his way through the corridor to the airlock. His two metal fingers clicked rapidly in anticipation. In the sub's forward lights, Deuce floated with the pulse capacitor. As he ascended rapidly through the water it was unlikely that spinners would be able to get to him in time. In case they did, the capacitor had already been charged for a small pulse. Then the decision to proceed would be up to Deuce.

Cindy watched the magnetometer. "So far, so good. I'm moving us outside pulse radius."

The sub rose and moved landward. After the pulse they would surface to establish radio contact with Deuce. Klaus poked his head in the door. "It's taking too long. We better go up."

Still watching her instruments, Cindy said, "It takes time to charge."

Klaus growled and ducked back to the hold. Another minute passed and the needle jumped. The lights dimmed, making her call to the back redundant, "Pulse activated, prepare to disembark."

The sub rose quickly as Cindy called out the depth, "Two hundred meters, one-fifty, one hundred meters, spinners on passive sonar, fifty meters, spinners dead in the water, ten meters, cyborgs to rafts, good luck boys and girls."

The sub popped out of the water amid the cyborg's battle calls. Through a film on the canopy, the oilrig rose out of the water like some steel monster. Charlie's heart constricted with nostalgia.

Over the radio, Deuce said, "I'm on the biomass belt. Everything looks quiet. I'm proceeding to the control room."

Klaus said, "Two planes in the air. They're circling on autopilot. The c.l.c. is knocked out."

Cyborgs in rubber rafts set out through choppy waters. Half headed to the rig. The others went to blow up spinners floating in the water with their electronic brains scrambled by the pulse. Someone screamed over the radio, "Spinner active! Coming up below us!" An explosion cut the transmission.

Klaus called out, "Tiny, what's going on?"

Cindy tapped at her sonar screen. "Look at these... six, seven, eight." She said into her headset, "Klaus, spinners in the water, eight active."

"Are they coming alive?"

"The ones knocked out are still dead. These are new."

"Where did they come from?"

The operation to mop up spinners turned into a full-scale battle. Cyborgs ran for their lives and returned fire on the c.l.c.'s torpedoes. Charlie snapped his fingers. "The pulse! That's how they did it!"

Sitting half out of her seat in frustration, Cindy snapped, "What are you talking about?"

"The c.l.c.'s couldn't stop a pulse, so they left some of their defenders inactive. They were set to turn on after the pulse went by."

Cindy tapped her headset. "Klaus, the rig might be alive. Advise retreat."

Charlie said, "If some of the spinners came awake, what about carryalls?"

Cindy said, "Deuce, what is your position?"

"I'm on the deck twenty meters from the building complex. Everything's quiet. Wait, there's movement in a pipe rack."

A burst of distant gunfire could be heard over Deuce's screams, "Carryall behind me! No, two. They have guns."

Deuce fired back. "They're all over the place. I'm running for the north side of the rig. Look for me in the water."

The radio cut out. Cindy said, "Retreat! Full retreat! Deuce may be in the water. The c.l.c. is still alive."

Spinners scrambled by the pulse regained function, and the cyborg retreat turned into a route. Cindy grabbed a machine gun and ran for the hatch. She yelled to Charlie, "Back away slowly and set for dive."

"Where are you going?"

"We need every gun up top. Watch for planes. If they drop bombs we're done."

Deuce didn't make it off the rig. As they steamed away, Charlie reassured the cyborgs that Deuce wouldn't be tortured. The machines only wanted him for biomass. The deck was soaked with blood. Charlie helped apply first aid, but couldn't look them in the eyes. Three dead, and every wound he saw might as well have been inflicted by his own hand. He knew the raid would be a disaster. Why hadn't he done more to talk them out of it?

Charlie slunk to the control room. Klaus was already there talking with Cindy in a low voice. As Charlie sank into the specialist's chair, he said, "I guess touching me wasn't such good luck after all."

Klaus said, "Nobody blames you, Charlie."

"I blame myself. I should have argued more strongly."

"Do you think we would have listened?"

"It was like I was wishing for something bad to happen."

"Maybe in your head, but not your heart. Besides, you shared the danger. You wouldn't have come along if you wanted total destruction."

"Not total destruction, just enough to prove me right."

"So how would you have planned the raid?"

"I'm not sure. I just knew they would be waiting for the pulse capacitor."

"Because it had been used successfully."

"Machines are logical and they expect us to be logical. The pulse worked once so they knew we would try it again. When I beat them in their simulations, it was usually when I did something illogical."

"Like what?"

"Like attacking their strongest link, not the weakest. The rigs are heavily defended against an attack from the outside."

"And against a pulse capacitor."

"We might do better attacking from the inside."

"If we were inside we would have already won."

Cindy said, "What do you mean Charlie?"

"I always wondered if the c.l.c. figured out how I got inside. I never told it that I was brought in on the biomass barge. If we could somehow get into a barge without the machines detecting us they would bring us right past the spinners."

Klaus grimaced. "Or the c.l.c. would let us sneak on, and then blow up the barge."

"It was just an idea."

"You do have a lot of ideas. I think everyone learned that today. We'll be several months recovering from this raid. When we're patched up and ready to fight again, how would you like to be in on the planning?"

"Only if I can fight as well."

Episode 6 – Land

Four months after their failed attack on an oilrig, the cyborg army set off to attack the same one again. Charlie said that a victorious c.l.c. wouldn't expect it. As he did before, Charlie sat in the copilot's chair. This time he cradled a machine gun on his lap. He slid the loading bolt back and forth.

"Would you put that away," Klaus growled. "You're making me nervous."

Charlie set it by his feet. "I don't have Wilbeforce to pet."

"Roy will take good care of him."

"It's not Wilbeforce I'm worried about."

Klaus glanced at the open hatch to the back. "If you have reservations, now is the time to voice them."

"It's a good plan," Charlie said weakly. "But nothing is perfect."

Sitting next to him in the pilot's seat, Cindy had not said a word the entire trip. Puffy eyes indicated that she had been crying. Klaus must have asked her to marry him again.

Charlie didn't push his plan strongly, but after his correct prediction of failure the last time, cyborgs deferred to his expertise. It wasn't fair, he was no seer. Anyone predicting machine victory would be right most of the time.

An hour after they set out from the Pearl Diver, Cindy spoke into her headset, "We're one kilometer from the rig. Diver teams have thirty minutes to swim to positions. The pulse will be followed five seconds later by the sub's horn. Good luck everyone. See you at rendezvous."

Just like before, a single diver would maneuver the pulse capacitor into range. Cyborgs waiting five hundred meters away would drive up after the pulse and destroy as many spinners as they could. They would retreat before the pulse-activated spinners could find them. Charlie rubbed sweaty hands on his pants. "How much time?"

Cindy said, "Ten minutes."

Klaus put a hand on his shoulder. "For good luck."

Charlie shook it off. "People touched me last time and they died."

Klaus said to Cindy, "We better go up."

Without acknowledging him directly, Cindy drove the sub slowly through pitch-black water. At three hundred meters they felt the pulse as a flickering of lights. Cindy sent the sub on a nose climb and sounded the sub's horn. When they popped out of the water, smoke and fire already poured from disabled spinners. Carryalls stood at the railing. As planes dove out of the sky, Cindy said, "Planes are active! Keep your heads up!"

Klaus said, "They're on automatic or the c.l.c. kept a second server idling through the pulse."

Additional carryalls crawled to the railing. For the c.l.c. they formed a multifaceted picture like the eyes of an insect. Charlie felt an intense personal connection to the c.l.c. that would soon be struggling to regain function.

Klaus said, "How many spinners are out?"

Cindy tapped at a sonar screen. "Eighteen at least."

Klaus said to Charlie, "Is that enough?"

"It should be."

Klaus thought a moment and then said over the radio, "Retreat! All cyborgs fall back to rendezvous."

Tiny said, "But Klaus, it's just sitting there wide open."

"Stick to the plan."

Cindy said, "Spinners active in the water. Fall back now!"

The sub dropped fast while Charlie thought furiously. Would eighteen be enough? The *Jules Verne* was well away. She lurked in the shallows near shore while the c.l.c. woke up. Charlie whispered, "I wonder if the c.l.c. will figure out what happened?"

Klaus whispered back, "How long do you think it will wait before it starts to rebuild?"

"The c.l.c.'s inventory programs are maintained separately from battle plans. Maintenance will take over after the Military stands down."

No cyborg had been killed during the fake assault. That alone should have told the c.l.c. to stay alert. Charlie counted on its inability to analyze a novel situation. The cyborgs waited all night in the stifling, closed-air of the sub. They ate dried food and tried to sleep, making low grumblings of mutiny. Charlie stayed in the cockpit with Cindy, eyes glued to the passive sonar. She whispered, "You better get some sleep."

Charlie wiped a dripping towel across his forehead. "My sinuses are plugged. Every time I close my eyes, it feels like I'm drowning."

When she shrugged, Charlie said, "Are you and Klaus fighting again?"

"We broke up."

"What? Why?"

"It wasn't fair to him. Klaus wants a family, and I can't bring children into this kind of world."

"You decided? I thought having children was automatic, like puppies or baby fleas. You have kids because genes are programmed to make that happen."

"I hope I have a little more choice in the matter than a dog or a flea."

"I don't know that you do. The species would die out if everyone felt like you."

"The species is not my problem. I can only think about my little ones suffering under freezing water, waiting for the final attack by machines."

"Maybe that could happen, or maybe your children will thrive and prosper. Maybe they'll be part of a solution. You can't give up for them in advance. Life will punch you a thousand times but there's always hope tomorrow."

"You watch the sonar. I'm going to try to sleep."

A state of tension can be held only so long before the mind slips into a world of fantasy. In the morning Klaus was practically jovial as he stepped into the control room. He whispered, "Well, Charlie, we're pinned to the shallows. If we move now the spinners will blow us out of the water."

"We still have the pulse capacitor."

"We would get one pulse off before spinners would be on top of us. If the c.l.c. doesn't move this morning, we'll try to get away in rafts. Some of us might make it."

"Land is a hundred meters away. We could climb up there and slip back into water far from the rig."

"So that's your game!" Klaus crowed in a harsh whisper. "You wanted to go to land all along so you trapped us against the beach!"

"Look," Cindy hissed. "A barge is coming."

Klaus turned his eyes from Charlie to the screen. "It's from our rig all right, and it will pass right next to us. I'll get a team in the water."

When Klaus left, Cindy gave Charlie a wink. "I had faith in you."

"The c.l.c. had to collect raw material to replace the spinners we destroyed."

After the demolition team disembarked, cyborgs still on the sub converged on the cockpit. Cindy looked back at the hatch. "Is this a mutiny?"

Curly pointed to the screen, "You'll see it here first, right?"

"Come on in."

Charlie was surprised to feel tentative touches on his shoulders. Maybe he had regained his status as a good luck charm. Fifteen minutes later the solid bulk of the barge cracked into multiple reflections. The cyborgs had busted it up. "That's it!" Curly screamed. "Take us up."

As Cindy's hand drifted over the ballast control, she said, "We're supposed to wait for visual confirmation."

Charlie tapped the radar. "I confirm."

"Good enough," Cindy said, taking the sub to the surface.

They moved sideways to avoid the two bobbing halves of the barge. Charlie counted carryalls plopping into the water, and warriors drafted to gather material for the new spinners. "The c.l.c. is going to be pissed," Charlie laughed, and then he saw the beach only a hundred meters away. "I'm going out to help."

"Be careful and stay out of the water. The horn will sound several seconds before the next pulse."

"What do I care? I don't have any chips."

Last in line to exit the hatch, Charlie climbed out to find cyborgs struck dumb, staring at the sandy beach, trees, and hills beyond. Charlie jerked a thumb towards open water. "Guys, spinners. Remember?" As he said it, Charlie couldn't tear his eyes off land. He could swim that distance in a few minutes.

The sub's horn sounded as the flaming bulk of the barge sank into the water. Cyborgs found safe positions and waited as the pulse turned their arms and legs into inanimate poles. "I'll check on Cindy," Charlie said, dipping back into the sub.

Charlie sat next to her rigid body until the ramjet inside her chest started spinning again. Cindy regained her color and tapped the headset. "Everyone okay?"

Klaus answered, "Another sixteen spinners knocked out. The rig is practically undefended."

"Should I go under?"

"Recharge the capacitor for another pulse. We'll approach from the surface."

Cindy smiled at Charlie. "With you on our side we'll finally push these machines out of the sea."

The rig was taken after a brief fight. Charlie climbed a rope ladder while listening to the c.l.c.'s communication frequency on a radio. Several minutes after the pulse it was struggling to achieve synchrony. Charlie wanted to be in the control room when it did.

As he walked across the deck, carryall warriors were sprawled on their sides with their brains pulled out. The rest had been lost on the barge. He entered the complex and jogged to the control room. Cyborgs were stripping components and light bulbs. Charlie felt a hush as he walked to one of the security cameras. The cyborgs watched in deference as he tapped the lens. "Hey, old-timer, remember me?"

The speaker remained silent. By the changing pitch on his radio, Charlie knew the c.l.c. was awake and analyzing. The cyborgs whirled when a maintenance robot flexed its legs. Charlie said, "No! It can't do anything to us now."

The room's speaker crackled, "Come to the carryall's camera. The security system is fried."

The cyborgs cringed at the voice. They closed in protectively as Charlie approached the maintenance carryall. Klaus said, "Careful."

Charlie stood in front of the camera. "Do you know me?"

"You are Charlie," the room speaker said.

"I am your worst scenario, a human that knows machines better than you know yourselves."

"RT-341 should not have let you live," the c.l.c. admitted.

"I was teaching you tactics."

"We would have learned on our own through real life battles."

"Once I was inside, there wasn't much that RT-341 could have done differently."

"Except turn itself off."

Cyborgs stared openmouthed at the exchange. Charlie said, "Do you know why I'm talking to you?"

"To gloat?"

"No, to offer you a deal. If machines leave the sea, humans won't come on land."

"You're afraid of us."

"Not me. I know that we can beat you on land eventually, but I brought the offer from our mayor."

"Your mayor can't bargain for every city."

"We can spread the word. To achieve peace, I think most would accept."

"There's no such thing as peace, Darwin's rule."

"You read Darwin?" Charlie said. The carryall swiveled and struck down hard with a straight blade.

Charlie yelped and jumped backwards. The blade missed his head by a centimeter but the tool sliced through Charlie's foot halfway between toes and ankle. Charlie fell on the floor gripping his foot in shock while Klaus's gun blew apart the carryall.

The room swirled about him like a dream. Cyborgs pulled his hands away to cut off his boot and tie a tourniquet. Others destroyed the stack. A painkiller injected into his neck wasn't working, Charlie thought desperately, until a closing tunnel of vision finally pinched off.

Charlie woke inside the sub. Drugs kept every neuron below his neck warm and happy, while a basketball-sized bandage was wrapped around his foot. The cyborgs sang in the hold around him; the mission was a rousing success. When she noticed his eyes flickering, Curly said, "Hey, he's up! Join the party, Charlie!" The cyborgs crowded around.

"My foot," Charlie croaked over a thick tongue.

Dex slapped his back. "Don't worry about that. We'll fix you up with a new plastic foot."

Tiny said, "It's about time you started looking like the rest of us."

Charlie's eyes widened. Why did Klaus and Cindy leave him in the hold? Dex said, "Don't look like that, mate. Your foot will never be cold again."

Charlie nodded and closed his eyes. To his relief the cyborgs rejoined their party, leaving him to suffer in peace.

Two months after the Santa Barbara Channel raid, Charlie hobbled down the corridor to Klaus's room. He knocked and waited until Klaus hopped to the door, minus his cybernetic arm and leg. "Charlie, come in, have a seat."

As the two made their way to the lower bunk, Klaus hopping and Charlie limping, Charlie said, "We are a pair of freaks aren't we?"

"If you would get a stack interface for that plastic foot, no one would even know you lost it."

"Dex already designed it."

"He wants you to have the best, we all do. After that raid you became one of us."

"Except that I won't mate the prosthetic to my brain."

Klaus spread his hand. "Your decision. Cindy baffles me as well, but it's no use arguing."

"Actually, that's part of the reason I'm here. We're waging the wrong battles. Humans will never get anywhere fighting for the water. The machines can take huge losses and just scavenge more material in the cities. To knock them back for good we have to take the war onto land."

"That's been proposed before, and never acted on because of the plague."

"People are already living there. I saw lights in the mountains and I saw bodies on the conveyor belt. They had dirt on their clothes and I found Wilby's scratching tree right next to them."

"They could have been swept up separately and mixed in a pile."

"We'll never know until we send someone to check it out. Drop me on the beach and come back in two months."

"You would never survive the machines alone."

"But we've got to find out!" Charlie stopped, and said, "What do you mean, alone?"

Klaus grinned. "It was just a matter of time. Did you see the way our friends stared at the beach? There was a longing there stronger than any fear. I'll talk to the mayor about putting together a small force, maybe six cyborgs."

"Including me," Charlie insisted.

"I can't promise that. You're our best mechanic and a valuable part of the planning group."

"Which is exactly why I should go. Both skills will be needed if we encounter machines on land."

Charlie had last worn his helmet four years earlier after waking up in a transport headed for the biomass ovens. It still had the same smell, Charlie thought wistfully, as he glided through dark water, pushing Wilbeforce before him in a sealed bag.

They moved underwater in case there were sentries. To reduce the risk of electronic detection, Charlie couldn't use his helmet's register, and the cyborgs had to shut down power to their prosthetics. As they clung to a pedal driven sled the one exception was Cindy's ramjet heart, insulated inside her chest.

While Tiny drove powerful legs against the pedals they measured progress only slowly against the tide. Five unpowered cyborgs hung desperately to the underwater raft. They felt the weight of childhood legends come back to haunt them. When Charlie's feet hit something solid, he pulled them up in alarm before realizing it was the beach.

Charlie dropped his legs and helped walk the sled forward until their heads broke water. Charlie pulled off his helmet and breathed deeply under a half-moon. The other cyborgs were doing the same, looking around the beach with idiotic grins. Still belted to the raft, Tiny's cybernetic arms hung down uselessly. "Can we turn on the power yet?"

Klaus hopped on one leg, splashing and studying the beach and trees beyond. "If land machines can detect our electronics, we'd better find out now while we can still swim away."

After powering limbs and sensors, the cyborgs felt more like themselves. They knelt to pull handfuls of wet sand out of the water. Klaus said, "Grab your packs and we'll sink the sled here."

Cindy said, "How will we find it again?"

"It's five meters out, and halfway between those two tall trees."

"I'll draw a mark in the sand just to make sure."

Klaus nodded, and as the group assembled their packs, Charlie wondered what was taking so long. No one wanted to be the first to climb the beach. "Oh my gosh! Wilbeforce must be going crazy by now."

Charlie unsealed the bag and turned on his power. Wilbeforce complained loudly, "Wilbeforce scared... I know Charlie... Wilbeforce scared..."

Charlie picked him up and walked towards the sand. As waves splashed from behind, Wilbeforce struggled higher until he reached Charlie's shoulders. Four meters from shore, Wilbeforce growled and leapt, leaving a deep scratch on Charlie's neck. Wilbeforce hit the water, jumped again, and tore up the sand into the trees ten meters away. Holding his neck, Charlie jogged after him, whispering loudly, "Wilby! Get back here!"

Klaus said, "Wilbeforce can always find us. The question is, can the machines?"

Charlie turned on his radio and scanned through the dial. "I don't hear anything." He set the volume low and put it in a shirt pocket. When he looked back, the cyborgs were staring.

Cindy pointed to his feet. "Look where you're standing, mate."

Charlie looked down at the sand and was overcome by a rush of emotion. "Land," he whispered, falling to his knees.

The cyborgs gathered around him as warmth in the buried sand spread through his hands and legs. Charlie looked up into their faces: Tiny, Klaus, Cindy, and Curly. "What do we do now?"

Tiny said solemnly, "I want to touch a tree."

"I guess first thing's first," Klaus sighed. "After we indulge our senses I propose we spend the night as close to the beach as possible."

For the first time in his life Charlie woke on land. The sun was still below forested hills to the east. Reflected blue light bounced off the sky and scattered through branches to the ground, gradually warming the earth through infinite photonic collisions. Charlie rubbed his arms while Tiny and Klaus returned from a small brick building. Charlie said, "Did you figure out what it is?"

Klaus said, "Bathroom."

"Not a machine in sight," Tiny added.

Cindy and Curly stirred under their blankets. Charlie jumped up. "I better use it first before they wake."

Tiny said, "There is a 'Men' and a 'Women'."

Charlie pulled on his boots, shaking his head in wonder. From the ground, Cindy said, "Did Wilbeforce come back last night?"

Charlie said, "Not yet," and walked away. It didn't rain during the night but a field overgrown with grass and yellow flowers wiped water across his legs as if he were walking in puddles. Charlie headed for a black walkway that curved around the field and arrived at the brick building on the far side. Charlie went inside and wondered how the waste was flushed out through the ground. It was not like the vast ocean; everything must be more complicated on land.

Standing at the basin, Charlie heard soft breathing behind him. He turned, and Charlie froze. A small white human stared at him. He had a pinched, deformed head with large front teeth and hands shaped like shovels. The creature was hairless and naked but didn't appear to be exactly man or woman.

"Host," Charlie whispered, pulling the name from the legends. Did it need to use the bathroom? Charlie zipped up slowly, and remembered another part of the legend, Host were man-eaters.

Charlie held up his hands and backed to the wall. The Host stood between him and the doorway. Wilbeforce was sitting in a nearby tree watching them. "You could have warned me!" Charlie thought fiercely.

Charlie wondered if he should shout out to the others, or maybe they had already been captured. The little guy didn't appear to be hostile. When Charlie lowered his hands, the Host said, "Hello."

Charlie screamed and jumped for the doorway. As he knocked the Host sideways, the radio went flying from his pocket. Charlie streaked through the field screaming, "Host! Host! Host!"

The cyborgs grabbed their weapons. When they got to the bathroom, the Host was gone. Klaus picked up Charlie's radio and turned the knobs. "Broken."

Cindy said, "So what do we do? Go look for this Host?"

Climbing down from the tree, Wilbeforce rubbed against Charlie's legs. Charlie said, "Which way did it go, boy?"

"Wilbeforce hungry."

Tiny nodded. "Tiny hungry too. I wish we could find this Host so we could eat it."

Charlie said, "You could not. It looks just like us, only small and... termite. That's what it was. I couldn't think of the name."

Klaus looked around the trees. "Well, termites aren't supposed to be dangerous."

Cindy said, "Where there are termites, there will be mantis warriors, so the stories say."

Klaus said, "We should at least find out if there's a nest around here."

"Do we bring our packs?"

"We'd better leave our camp here. I got a feeling this experiment could fall apart at any time."

Charlie said, "Do you think the city would let us back before the six-week quarantine?"

Cindy said, "You told them to blow us up if we tried to return early."

"Then we'll go to another city," Klaus growled. "I just want to stay near the water."

The cyborgs traveled in a close group, exploring the outer reaches of the wilderness. They found a sign reading, *Shoreline Park*, and a vast jungle of streets and crumbling buildings beyond. The cyborgs stood silently, lost in their own thoughts. The vast scale was impressive, but Charlie could feel only rage at the sight of the dead civilization. Cindy said, "Should we look inside the buildings?"

There was no movement in the streets or inside broken windows until Wilbeforce took after a rat. Charlie jogged after him and the others followed, ducking through an empty doorway into a bookstore. Piled on the floor, tens of thousands of dusty books easily surpassed the Pearl Diver's own poor library many times over. Having lost the rat through a hole in the wall, Wilbeforce sniffed at mildewing piles of paper and glue. Charlie said, "All the collected wisdom of our species."

Klaus looked at the others and raised his one remaining eyebrow. "I wonder where the bodies are, I mean after the plague struck?"

Tiny said, "Host or machines got 'em most likely."

Charlie picked up Wilbeforce. "I bet their pets ate them after they died. Serves them right for leaving them behind."

Cindy touched his arm. "Charlie, what's wrong?"

He nodded around the room. "This is our legacy, a ruined bookstore in a ruined city."

"We aren't gone yet, Charlie. We survived in the sea. That's the beauty of our species, adaptability."

The cyborgs spent the rest of the morning exploring shops in the city. On the Pearl Diver, the objects they found, clothes, toys, and furniture, represented a vast fortune. When word got back, there would be countless forays into the city for wealth. Maybe that was for the best. Greed was the greatest motivator in the world. If machines got in the way, they would have to be eliminated.

As they headed back to the park for lunch, there was a faint humming sound. Charlie reached automatically for his radio before remembering it was smashed. Klaus scanned the sky as they stood in the shadow of a bank. "We'd better get inside," he said, when the sidewalk exploded around them.

Silver ball bearings bounced from the ground like gunshot, scattering cyborgs in all directions. Through a choking dust of powdered cement, Charlie crawled through the bank window. The plane that dropped the load headed south. Curly lay still in the street, her silver skull smashed. Tiny crawled towards her, one mechanical arm hanging limp. "Oh Curly," he cried, trying to gather her body with one good arm.

Cindy touched his shoulder. "We can't fix this one."

Tiny nodded, and Klaus said, "Let's get her back to camp before the carryalls come."

After Charlie fixed the connection on his arm, Tiny insisted on carrying Curly's body. Mechanical arms stretched out before him like the prongs of a forklift. They set out along the street, one less in number. If only he hadn't panicked when he saw the termite, Charlie thought darkly. His radio wouldn't have been broken and he might have heard c.l.c. instructions to the approaching plane. They followed city streets to the park and over trails towards camp. At the last rise, Klaus waved them down with a fierce gesture.

Tiny lay Curly's body in the grass and they crept forward. Along the sloping hill to the beach, two carryalls picked through their camp, opening packs, and turning over blankets. Seeing his pack of smoked tuna, Charlie's stomach growled. Klaus glared at him and waved the group back to the bushes.

"What do we do?" Cindy whispered. "They got our food."

"And our helmets," Klaus said. "We're stuck on land until the *Jules Verne* returns."

"In six weeks," Charlie added.

Tiny said, "It looks like we may get a taste of Host after all."

"Or they will get a taste of us," Klaus said. "We still got our weapons and we are in survival mode. I propose we find a place in the city to hide. We'll say our goodbyes to Curly now and pick her up on the way back to the *Verne*."

"If the machines don't find her," Tiny grumbled.

Klaus had nothing to say to that. The cyborgs returned to the streets and kept moving inland. Beyond the business strip were rows of houses. With yards overgrown in weeds they were still more beautiful than any undersea apartment Charlie had ever seen. The cyborgs explored a second-floor bathroom bigger than their rooms in the Pearl Diver. Charlie flopped on a gigantic bed. "They lived like kings."

Cindy peeked through a curtain. "Klaus, there's a forest not far from here."

Klaus and Tiny walked out of the bathroom, limbs humming in electronic precision. Klaus nodded through the window. "That's probably where the Host nest is. If we could grab one from the edges we could bring it back here to cook."

Charlie sat up sharply. "You haven't seen them, you might as well eat me."

"Surely we would eat Wilbeforce before you."

"Fine, make a joke."

Cindy said, "It's not a joke, Charlie. We are in bad situation, and it could get a whole lot worse."

Klaus said, "Let's just go take a look. Maybe we'll find a dog or something."

From the house it was a short walk through residential streets to Hondo Valley Park. Bigger than Shoreline Park and covered in dense forest, it could hold any number of nests. Charlie said, "We'll be on top of them before we even know it."

Klaus checked his machine gun and the two-shot pistol built into his hand. "Get ready for a fight then."

The cyborgs jogged across Harbor Hills Drive and plunged through head high bushes. Under layers of canopy they were lost in darkness before traveling three meters. Tiny took the lead, snapping branches with steel hands and pushing forward on powerful legs. Cindy came next, covering him with her gun, and then Charlie holding Wilbeforce who wanted no part of the jungle. Klaus brought up the rear, walking backwards to cover their tracks.

When they had gone a hundred meters, Tiny cried out and then turned back. "Sorry, false alarm."

The others crowded around a machine crouched behind a tree. Its steel frame was rusted through. "It startled me," Tiny said embarrassed.

Cindy ran her finger along a blade on a pivoting knife board. "Evil."

Klaus said, "It lay in wait for a passing body. I wonder why it's still here."

"Maybe the battery ran out and the c.l.c. lost track."

Klaus motioned Tiny forward. "I see light ahead."

They climbed a hill pushing against bushes. At the ridge they could see down over the trees to an open field several hundred meters away. A small stream wound through the middle. Tiny licked his lips. "I bet it's fresh water."

Cindy pointed to a small group of Host climbing out of a hole on the far side. Klaus croaked, "They look like kids. What are we doing here?"

Charlie said, "I knew you couldn't eat them."

"Not that. What are we doing on land at all? If it's full of machines and those hideous creatures, I say let them have it."

Cindy said, "That's really not our decision, Klaus. We're here only to see if the plague is still active."

Charlie pointed downhill. "I think that question has just been answered."

Exiting from the same hole as the Host, a fully dressed woman charged out of the ground. Cradling a dripping canvas bag, she ran over the field to the north. A half-dozen Host jogged after her, and then gave up before the woman even disappeared into the trees. "What was that about?" Cindy said.

Klaus said, "Who cares? Charlie was right, humans live on land. We can go back now and report."

Charlie said, "We don't have helmets. I don't like the idea of floating on the surface with spinners for six weeks."

"I would almost take that chance, but you're right. Let's get back to the house and don't loosen your grip on dinner, I mean Wilbeforce."

"Let's follow the human. She'll have food and a safe place to live."

"And just why would they share with us?"

"We're their long lost cousins from the sea. I'm sure they'll be thrilled to see us."

Klaus shrugged. "It's worth a try. We'll go south around the field to stay far from the nest."

After thirty minutes of hot scratchy work trampling brush, the cyborgs reached the opposite side of the valley. Finding boot prints on a trail they moved quicker. Tiny led the way until they reached a rocky ravine sloping to the right. He pointed at a body laying at the bottom, an oozing bag at her side. "It's her."

Charlie said, "She must have slipped."

He started down to help her, when Klaus grabbed his arm. "No, I'll go."

Klaus skidded down the slope, cradling the machine gun in one hand and watching the trees and rocks around him. At the bottom of the ravine he started towards the body when an arrow pierced his gun arm.

The woman scrambled into a ditch while arrows flew from the trees. Some stuck in Klaus's flesh and some bounced from prosthetics. Klaus curled to keep his cyborg side up while Tiny and Cindy returned fire. Charlie scrambled down the hill, waving his arms. "Stop! Stop! We're human!"

Cindy shouted, "Charlie, no!" but the arrows stopped.

Charlie ran towards Klaus, and yelled to the ditch, "Help me! He's hurt."

A girl about his own age poked her head up. She looked to the trees for confirmation and met Charlie at Klaus's still body. Charlie rolled him over, exposing the steel nose, cheek, and camera lens. The girl pointed. "Human?"

"Yes," Charlie said. "His face was lost fighting the machines."

The girl watched while Charlie tied bandages to stop the bleeding. Klaus groaned and opened his eye. "Do I get any more metal?"

"All flesh wounds."

When Klaus spoke, the girl approached and smeared the blood on his forearm. "No trick?"

"No trick," Charlie said.

Wilbeforce wandered down from the trees flexing his cybernetic claw. He sniffed at Klaus's arm, and said, "Wilbeforce hungry."

The sight and sound of a talking cybernetic cat overcame the caution of the others. A half-dozen ragged humans emerged from the trees. Charlie yelled, "Tiny, Cindy, come on. Klaus is going to need help."

Charlie touched his ear where it had been severed by the carryall. Sliding on the rock it had started bleeding again. Over the body of a fallen comrade the groups studied each other. The cyborgs had short-cropped hair and advanced weapons. The humans were, dirty, longhaired, and clutched bows and arrows. Two of the humans held bags like the one on the ground. Cindy pointed at the leaking goo. "What is that?"

The girl who had played hurt looked at a large male and then back to Cindy. "Protein paste from the hive. We take it for the village."

Tiny's face fell. "That's what you eat?"

"Among other things. We grow vegetables and raise rabbits." The large male waved her quiet.

Charlie looked at him. "My name is Charlie. These are Klaus, Cindy, Tiny, and Wilbeforce. We came from the ocean to see if the plague was still active."

The humans looked at each other smiling, but the big male said nothing. Finally the girl said, "My name is Dawn. We thought humans living in the sea was just a legend."

Charlie said, "And we thought humans living on land was just a legend. Look, our friend is hurt. Could we take him to your village and treat him?"

The leader said nothing until they heard the mechanical whine of an airplane. He searched the sky. "We better get under the trees."

Four of the humans helped carry Klaus towards the trees on the far side of the ravine. Dawn said, "Our village is north of here about three kilometers."

Charlie took Klaus's pack. "You came all this way to steal food?"

She picked up the sack of protein paste. "They fight back if we go to the same hive too often."

Charlie thought about the termite in the bathroom, and the Host giving Dawn a halfhearted chase. "They don't attack you?"

"The worst I ever got was a stag horn in my hip and that's when I got too close to his queen."

Charlie shook his head. "But the legends... The Host wars..."

"The survivors of those wars figured it out. If they left the Host alone, the Host left them alone."

"And we were going to grab one to eat."

"That's still done in some parts, but those villages are sometimes wiped out in retaliation. It's like the machines. If we stay away from their factories, they don't give us too much trouble. That's why we live in the mountains where the carryalls don't move very well."

"You never thought about living in the cities?"

"The machines would attack us there."

"Then fight back."

"We only have bows and knives."

"Not if you built guns."

"We don't use machines. That would make us like them."

Hiking along roads and through empty neighborhoods it took an hour to cover the three kilometers to the Los Padres Mountains. Red-faced and sweating, Charlie climbed the final hill into a sand wash canyon. The humans, four of whom carried Klaus, ended the march as easily as they began with long sure strides. Even carrying a heavy pack, Dawn wasn't winded. As they talked, Charlie found the humans tough but superstitious. Charlie could only wonder what they thought about cyborgs.

The humans occupied tents and hovels in the rocks. A tangled green net stretched over the trees formed a camouflaged common area of almost twenty square meters. Charlie didn't know how it could fool the c.l.c.'s planes, but judging by the number of babies in camp, they were not only surviving but thriving.

The cyborgs were met at the netting entrance and led off separately to be cared for. Charlie resisted being divided, but the villagers seemed genuinely friendly, and Dawn took Charlie's hand. She led him to a barrel, and dipped a rag into the dirty water. "Your ear is bleeding."

"If you put that on, it will get infected."

When the girl frowned in rebuke, Charlie held the rag to his head. "I'd better see about Klaus."

Dawn held his arm. "We have a doctor."

"Your doctor won't know how to work the prosthetics."

She pulled him back. "They'll get you if they need help. Tell me about life under the sea."

Charlie let himself be pulled to the sand where he began slowly and completely to spill his guts. Dawn listened in wonder as he described his childhood in the harvester three hundred meters under the ocean. She stroked his arm while he described the machine attack and his father's death. She laughed when he explained how the carryalls had become his friends, and she held his hand while he described his rescue and life with the cyborgs. When he finished, Dawn said, "I'm an orphan too. The machines got my parents when I was three."

"Have you forgiven them?"

"The machines?"

"No, your parents. Why didn't they plan better? Why did they leave us?"

Dawn pulled his head to her shoulder as Charlie sobbed. Released at last, tears of grief rolled down his cheeks. Dawn patted his hair until Wilbeforce trotted by, a young girl chasing after his mechanical tail. Charlie sniffed and pulled back in embarrassment. "I guess our parents did the best they could. Every day life hit them in the face with a thousand choices. It would be unfair to judge now."

"That sounds about right."

Cornered in a tree with dirty children underneath, Wilbeforce let out a plaintive howl. Charlie smiled. "He's a real cat at last. Why do you have so many kids here?"

"To fill the earth." Dawn leaned close. "Are you going to stay with us?"

"Until Klaus is strong enough to travel."

"Why go back at all?"

"We have to tell the others. When they find out that they can live here, they will come back to land someday. There are four million people in the oceans ready to retake their birthright."

"And what about you?"

Charlie held her close. "I'll be leading the way."

Excerpt from Book 6: Spegellandet

Episode 1 – The Flying Fortress

Dressed in rags Arno crawled facedown along the floor to a bowl of water. In the dim light of the jail cell window, Simon and Garfunkle drank at his bowl, just as he had expected. With a triumphant gleam in his eye, Arno raised his hands. The movement was enough to trigger a growl from his empty stomach.

The cockroaches took off instants ahead of Arno's hands. Simon was his. Garfunkle crawled through the bars minus two legs. Arno chuckled low in his throat and stuffed the struggling giant cockroach into his mouth.

When the door clicked, Arno dropped flat to the floor. He pretended to sleep with his head in a pool of water sloshed from the bowl. The lights went on and two machines scuttled in on six steel legs. All-in-all Arno preferred the cockroaches.

One of the carryalls stood guard at the door while the other stepped across the room and opened the cell door. Still feigning sleep Arno calculated the leap he would have to make over the first machine. The second would be alerted but Arno would just have to face that problem when it came.

Arno moved like lightning. Grunting as he leaped over the waist high-carryall, his wrist was just as quickly snagged in a steel pincher. When Arno beat at the limbs and lenses, his other wrist was snagged. He tried to twirl. He thought he could smash the smaller carryall against the bars but its little steel body was surprisingly heavy.

The carryall headed for the door with Arno in tow by his wrists. As a last useless gesture Arno let his body go limp, sweeping the floor with tattered clothing as he was dragged away. The second carryall fell in line behind him and all three moved down the corridor. The thing Arno hated most was the complete indifference of the machines. He had tried to escape, but they weren't angry, or even aroused. They were just completing an assigned task as if he did not even exist.

As they proceeded through the heart of the fortress, Arno changed strategy. The machines were too strong to fight so he would cooperate. They plucked him from his forest home for some reason. They had need of him and therefore he had leverage. It gave him some hope when he climbed to his feet, and the jailer's cuffs raised accordingly. The machines were responsive to his actions.

Arno was led inside another small room off the corridor. He changed strategy again, struggling while they locked him into an interrogation chair. The cuffs never released. The carryall holding him transferred its pinchers smoothly into the chair's arms. The carryalls crawled out, legs clicking on the metal floor.

Arno searched the room for some clue as to the future. There was no furniture besides the chair but there was another door opposite the one they entered. Would his death come through that door on polished steel legs?

Arno dozed until some time later the door opened. He was slightly disappointed that it was the same one he had been dragged through. What terrible secret lay behind the other? When he turned his head, Arno was surprised to find a human backing through the door. He was even more surprised when the man turned, revealing a tray of food.

Arno looked up gratefully, and then recoiled from a ball of blinking lights, growing off the side of the man's head like a tumor. "Don't be alarmed. I mean you no harm."

"What are you?" Arno squeaked.

The man smiled. "I am not a 'what', but a 'he'. I am Elliot."

"But that thing!"

"An interface to a stack register. Am I too horrible to look at?"

The smell of steaming rice shaded Arno's answer. "I was just startled."

Elliot set the tray on the floor. "You have never seen humans with machine parts before?"

Arno could not repress an involuntary shudder. "No."

Elliot searched his eyes and then said, "If I let you loose to eat, you would not try to get away?"

"Where could I go?"

When Elliot unlocked the cuffs, Arno squatted at the tray stuffing hot rice and fistfuls of corn into his mouth. It was Elliot's turn to recoil. "I guess you haven't eaten in some time."

Arno didn't bother to answer until he had scooped up the last kernel and grain in dirt-stained fingers. "What am I doing here?"

"You were caught near the coastal mountains."

"Yes."

"We need information," Elliot started and then cocked his head to the side.

"What is it?" Arno said, looking around. He heard nothing until moments later heavy footsteps marched down the corridor. "Another machine?" Arno whispered.

Elliot gave a quick shake of his head. He didn't move until the door swung open. Another human stood framed in the doorway, massive shoulders nearly brushing the sides as he pushed through. With a look of disgust he pointed at Arno. "What is that vermin doing out of the chair?"

In running shorts and a black tank top, the man's muscles dripped sweat as if he had just come from the gym. Only slowly did Arno spot the same ball of lights blinking in his skull. When the man saw Arno's reaction he marched over as if to strike him. The giant turned on Elliot instead. "I hope you haven't started the interrogation without me."

"No, Howell, he needed to be fed."

Howell grunted. He glanced at the open door to the hallway as if daring Arno to run. When Arno cowered in submission, Howell nodded and licked his lips. "What is your name?"

"Arno."

"How many people are in your tribe?"

"About fifty."

"How long did you live in the forest?"

"Many years. I was born inland but my family moved when a factory was built near our farm."

Howell nodded, seemingly pleased with the extra information. Arno did want to please him. Arno sat when Howell indicated the chair but the cuffs were not attached. Hands on hips, Howell stood in front of him while Elliot stood further back. Howell said, "Have you ever seen a cyborg?"

"A what?"

"A human with machine parts."

"You two are the first."

"Have you heard of cyborgs living in the sea?"

"No."

"Have you heard of a cyborg army attacking factories?"

"No."

"Liar!" Howell slapped him across the face.

Stunned by the speed of the attack, Arno could only hold his cheek as numbness slowly gave way to pain in his jaw. Elliot stepped forward. "Howell, he doesn't know."

Howell licked his lips. "A cyborg army attacked a factory just five kilometers from your forest!"

Arno shook his head. His mouth hurt as he answered, "We never leave our camp, too dangerous. What do you want?!"

Howell grabbed Arno by the wrist dragging him to the other door. He punched a code. The panel slid open, revealing the outside of the fortress, a patch of sky, pink and orange in the late afternoon dusk five kilometers above the ground.

Arno quaked in fear. "What do you want?"

As effortlessly as a machine, Howell swung Arno out the door by his wrist and let him go. As Arno's screams faded, Elliot rushed forward. "What did you do that for?"

Howell looked over the lands far below, answering calmly, "He asked me what I wanted."

"But he didn't know anything about cyborgs!"

"I know that. What's your problem? He's not one of us."

"He was the last unaltered subject," Elliot whined.

"Sometimes I think you are not one of us."

Elliot glanced at the door. "Are you going to throw me out too?"

"Would you like to take a trip?"

"I just dare you. How would you explain that to Diotima?"

Howell sneered, but the mention of their mistress gave him pause. "You would love for me to solve all your problems, wouldn't you?"

Elliot shrugged and took a step towards the open door. Howell's eyes widened. When Elliot turned his back to him, Howell growled and stalked out of the room. Elliot stood at the threshold of the door, arms braced to the sides like wings. The sky was so beautiful. Living inside their flying fortress Elliot did not see it nearly as much as when he had lived on land.

Elliot stroked the machine implant in his skull. He was disgusted by the horror he had become, Arno had been right to recoil. Elliot sniffed at the wind racing past his nose. For two years, Diotima's fortress had not set down. That was the last time Elliot felt solid earth under his feet.

"What are you thinking?"

Elliot jumped and looked around the room. He was never sure whether the voice came from outside or inside his head. "Nothing, Diotima."

"What did you learn from the savage?"

"Nothing. He knew nothing."

"Then we will have to catch a cyborg for ourselves."

"Yes, Diotima."

"Send the savage to the operating room. There is a new interface I want you to try."

"The savage expired, an accident."

Diotima's chuckle flooded Elliot's brain. "Don't tell me Howell was there as well?"

"By your order," Elliot said, getting mad.

"Never mind that, Elliot. We have a world full of savages."

"Yes, Diotima."

"Pick the healthiest subject from the hospital for my interface."

"What about Princess?"

"Not yet," Diotima snapped. Elliot actually felt heat coursing through the circuits in his head. "The science must be perfect before we use her."

Elliot said, "Yes, Diotima," but he had already felt the withdrawal of contact. Elliot stood a long time staring out the open door as skies faded to purple. How many times in those minutes did he will his legs to jump? Did Diotima control him through the interface in his brain, or was he merely monitored as promised?

Elliot sighed and slid the door closed. He walked the width of the fortress to a hospital built into the starboard wing. Ten beds were filled with patients in varying states of intensive care. Monitors beeped and heart/lung machines hummed taking over the processes of living as toxins from failing interfaces leaked into their systems.

That was one reason Diotima was so anxious to catch a cyborg. The humans had found a way to merge the two species. Of all the attempts Diotima made to graft stack registers into human brains, only Elliot and Howell survived, and Elliot feared that both he and Howell were going mad.

At the first bed Elliot found that Susan had expired. Her voice box had been replaced with a mechanical pressure transducer, but all she had ever been able to manage were whispers and squeaks. Skin along the sides of the titanium box had blackened and curled, exposing red basal membrane underneath. Always at the boundaries, mechanical grafts were recognized and avoided as alien.

Diotima had been trying different combinations of coatings, injected drugs, and electric stimulation to mimic neural pathway transmissions. The most successful attempts were full replacements. An entire mechanical leg was accepted much easier than a single plastic tendon or memory-wire hamstring muscle. The body seemed to get confused when overwhelmed with technology. Little pieces it could recognize and fight.

Elliot disconnected monitors and pulled the sheet over Susan's head. He transferred her to a gurney and wheeled her through the room under reproachful eyes of the other experiments. Elliot felt guilty when they stared at the blinking lights in his head. Were they jealous of his success or angry that his survival inspired Diotima's further testing?

In the rear sections of the fortress Elliot wheeled Susan to waste disposal. He slid her body out from under the sheet and into a bin. How light she had become. Elliot would feel hypocritical praying for her soul so he just hit a button releasing her to the sky and back to the earth from where she came. Elliot headed back to the hospital with the gurney. In one section of the quiet corridor where Diotima had no cameras, he hid Susan's bed sheet underneath his jacket.

From his perch ten meters off the ground Charlie swept aside the branch of a noble fir. With an unobstructed view to the valley floor, Charlie studied the factory. A hundred meters long, fifty meters wide, and two stories tall, the machine factory was the copy of ten thousand others located throughout the western United States. Scavenging material from empty towns and cities, the factories would reproduce themselves until they filled the world.

A truck arrived with biomass for the furnace. At one time the factories would only extract energy from the bodies of Homo Insectus mutants, so the legends said, but the truck's bin was full of dusty two by fours, newspapers, and dead tree branches. Charlie had seen carryalls digging at the edges of garbage dumps and remote controlled construction vehicles tearing down houses. If the machines worked long enough, the world would be reduced to forests and factories.

The machines were so efficient, they started to push into the sea. Building factories on abandoned oilrigs, the machines attacked undersea human communities. The cyborgs destroyed some, forcing the other factories to fight back.

After a plague wiped out humans on land a hundred years earlier, survivors were afraid to come out of the water. The few who did were never heard from again, probable victims of the plague, machines, or Host. Coastal fighting between machines and human cyborg armies could have gone on forever except for one group that did come back.

Leading four cyborgs and a cat, a boy of fourteen, a refugee from a destroyed undersea city found a village of humans surviving in the mountains. With the plague no longer a danger, four million humans living underwater were free to take the fight onto land.

As carryalls unloaded the vehicle, Charlie turned on his radio and scanned the dial. He found frequencies that the factory's complex logic controller used to direct its robots. Charlie listened intently to the whistling data stream. He couldn't identify individual commands within the chaos, but years of living on a machine factory gave him a sixth sense into the inner workings of the register. Charlie scratched his cat who sat next to him on the branch. "What do you think, Wilby?"

Wilbeforce sniffed at a patch of sap. Charlie nodded. "Me too. It doesn't suspect a thing."

Climbing from the tree, Charlie's plastic foot slipped on a branch, sending him crashing down the last three meters to a bed of pine needles. Charlie blinked and looked up into the faces of his friends. Klaus was a cyborg, half his face replaced by steel. Cindy, Klaus's girlfriend, had a machine heart, and Dawn, his own girlfriend of six months. "My foot slipped," Charlie said sheepishly.

Not even his girlfriend looked sympathetic. Voice tense, Klaus said, "The team is ready. Can you lead the attack?"

Charlie flexed arms and legs. "Nothing broken."

Cindy pointed to his radio's cracked speaker. "Except that."

"Not again," Charlie breathed. He scrambled upright and limped back towards camp. "As soon as I get a replacement we can go."

Klaus said, "That'll take ten minutes. What can it tell us?"

Charlie looked hard at the cyborg. "I shouldn't have to remind you."

"Go ahead then," Klaus growled. "But each minute we delay is another minute we risk detection."

"This is the easy one, Klaus. After today, the machines will know we're here."

"Maybe it's better that we fail now then."

"Why would you say that?"

Klaus looked around the forest. "Everything is strange here."

"Is that all? You'll get used to it."

"Some of the other cyborgs feel the same way. Once we get our people established, we might return to the water."

"You complain all day about the water, the fungus, the cold, the taste of fish."

Klaus held a bare forearm under the sunlight. "It's the devil we know."

The complex logic controller had trees and bushes cut back a hundred meters from factory walls. Any charge over land would give it time to close doors tight and get bombers in the air. With a truck full of cyborgs, Charlie hoped to get inside the factory before the c.l.c. even knew there was an assault. If they could shut the stack register down before it sent alarms to other factories, the attack could be repeated down the road.

Charlie sweated in the back with the rest. It was just like the trucks that the c.l.c. used to haul biomass, but this one would not respond to radio queries. The question was, what would the c.l.c do about it? In the hot dark air Charlie turned up the radio in his pocket. As the truck lumbered slowly down the hill towards the factory, even untrained cyborgs noticed a change in the register's data stream. Klaus gripped Charlie's arm. "Trouble?"

"The problem is still with Maintenance. Probably ordering an overhaul on the truck."

Klaus turned an infrared camera lens eye on Charlie. "I'm glad you're on our side."

Charlie blushed in the dark. "Just get ready to move. If the situation is sent to Defense we'll have about five seconds to get into the garage."

Klaus clicked his safety off, setting loose a chain reaction of weapons' checks. The truck pulled up to the garage, turned, and backed through the roll down door. The cyborgs held their breaths while a team of six-legged maintenance carryalls descended on the truck. "What's keeping them," Klaus growled as one of the beasts crawled across the roof over their heads.

A shoulder fired missile streaked down from the trees, slamming into the factory's communication dishes. Even inside the garage, the truck was rocked by the explosion. Klaus kicked open the door. "Move! Move!"

Cyborgs poured into the garage firing at defenseless carryalls. Leaving Charlie safe in the truck until it was over, Klaus jogged back. "There's no door into the factory!"

Charlie grunted acknowledgment and climbed down from the back.

"We got to take the stack out!" Klaus said with more urgency.

Charlie looked around the garage and pointed to the wall. "There. Rungs to the ceiling."

"So? There's no door."

"Cut one. I'm sure you'll find a corridor beyond."

Klaus shook his head in agitation but he passed on the order. While a giant cyborg named Tiny worked with a torch, factory carryalls arrived at the garage door. Cyborgs shot at them as they poked camera lenses around the corner. "I'm liking this less and less," Klaus said. "The c.l.c. is still active."

There was a loud clang as a heavy metal disc hit the floor. Tiny poked his head up through the hole. "There's a corridor."

Klaus looked at Charlie. "How did you know?"

Charlie pointed to the open garage door. "Leave three to cover our backs. Everyone else into the factory."

Klaus signaled and followed Charlie up the rungs. They had to bend over double to jog through the corridor. It ended at another ladder down to an empty room with several doorways. When Charlie climbed down, Tiny was already returning from a short reconnaissance. He hooked a thumb over his shoulder. "Bathrooms. They got showers and toilets back there."

Trying not to show surprise, Charlie said, "It's in the legends. These factories were built for people to live in. The stupid c.l.c.'s keep adding toilets and bunks just because they're in the plans."

Klaus said, "What about the ladder to nowhere?"

"I guess mistakes pile up after a while, like genetic damage that doesn't get repaired."

Klaus said, "Tell me the truth. When you said to cut the ceiling you didn't really know there was a corridor up there did you?"

Charlie smiled and said to cyborgs descending the ladder, "We don't want anything from this c.l.c. Blast any server you find." Charlie listened to the radio as the c.l.c. sent out last desperate orders. "I'll call you when the stack is dead."

The cyborgs split up, running through the empty factory. They fired at blinking lights and the few remaining carryalls. Charlie followed Klaus down a long corridor lined with rooms. Klaus blasted a maintenance carryall as it tried to crawl away, legs slipping on the steel plating. Standing over the smoking shell, he said, "Another tool user. We haven't found one warrior."

"There's been no one to fight for years. Doesn't make sense to keep warriors."

"It looks like an easy campaign."

"The machines learn fast, and even if this one didn't get a call out, the other c.l.c.'s will notice a gap in their network. They'll investigate."

"That's why we have to establish a beachhold before they organize."

Charlie stepped inside a room and looked around the walls. He swung down one of the two bunk beds, complete with foam mattress. Klaus folded down a table opposite the bunks. "The rooms are small just like in our city."

"Do you think our people could get used to living in these factories?"

"That's the plan, isn't it?"

"That's our plan, but it looks like that was the plan all along."

"Then why do the machines fight?"

"Something went wrong. These towns were built for us. If there was only some way we could make the machines understand that."

Tiny yelled from the courtyard, "Klaus, get out here!"

In the factory's central courtyard cyborgs gathered around a massive rocket. The main body sank thirty meters into the ground. The top of the rocket was missing and the factory roof was open to blue sky. The factory was waiting for a crane to lower the final piece of the rocket. Klaus peered down the well into darkness. "What the hell?"

"There was nothing about this in the legends." Charlie looked at their cyborg mechanic. "Dex? What's it for?"

The mechanic scratched his head. "The nose cone is missing. If we find the payload it would answer your question. Absent that, it looks like a two-stage intercontinental ballistic missile."

"Intercontinental?"

"Or possibly interplanetary if the payload is small enough. If the c.l.c. hasn't been scrambled maybe we can get something out of the database."

Charlie nodded. "I'll get on it."

Tiny cleared his throat, and nodded to the empty lunch tables scattered around the courtyard walls. "Begging your pardon, Charlie, but you said we would eat after the factory was secure."

"Of course. Remember that hive we passed in the forest? Dawn is going to show us how to eat off the land by raiding Host protein stores."

Diotima hated the sound of her metal feet as she clunked across the floor. It was not so much the awkwardness as the constant reminder that she had not achieved success. An entire galaxy waited to be conquered, if only she could figure out this last piece of engineering. Machines had already started to take over the Earth, but only after it had been filled with register chips and refined metals.

There would be other worlds with the same infrastructure, but not enough to keep an interstellar expansion going. Diotima had to minimize the amount of metal needed to conquer a world. She had to figure out how to fuse machinery with biology. The final clue might be found among the cyborg armies attacking her factories on the coast.

Diotima stood before a full length mirror in her room, admiring the perfect form of her body. Ten times as strong as a human, metal and plastic had been molded into the shape of a young woman. Diotima called herself "the warrior princess" after the girl who had first given her register programs intuition and desire.

Powered by batteries, alas, the Warrior Princess could only thrive and multiply in a technological society. To conquer the organic galaxy Diotima needed to perfect a brain, and this is where she was sadly lacking.

Diotima leaned close to the mirror. Camera lenses poked through the eye sockets examining a decomposing human head strapped onto the shoulders of her perfect mechanical body. Hair fell out in patches, and yellow-green skin sagged around the eyes and ears. A thin line of blood around the severed neck had long ago turned black and blown away. Diotima never expected it to survive, but she wanted it there as a reminder of her goal.

Diotima took a brush from the dresser and brushed long, black tresses gingerly so they wouldn't fall out of the head. Elliot knocked on the door and entered without waiting for an answer. Through the mirror Diotima could see Elliot repress a shudder. "You called?"

Diotima lay down the brush and turned. "I wanted to talk with you personally. I hope my appearance is not too unsettling."

Elliot swallowed hard. "Of course not, Diotima."

"I would have spoken by radio but this is of a sensitive nature. I didn't want Howell to eavesdrop."

When Elliot nodded, a drop of sweat rolled off the end of his nose. Diotima's warning programs began analysis. Not for the first time, she suspected that Elliot might be hiding something. Distracted for the moment, Diotima hesitated and then said, "The mission to Japan was successful."

Elliot blinked. "That's why you called?"

"You counseled against this plan."

"You are the mistress."

"Yes," Diotima said wryly. "I am. A plane is returning. I want you to start renovating the genetics lab in Colorado."

"In person?"

"The remote carryalls will suffice. I called you here to remind you that time is growing short."

"I'm doing everything I can."

"Are you? I still don't have my cyborgs."

"They don't have the brain linkages you seek."

"They must have complex neural links to their prosthetics. I want you to grab some as soon as possible."

"Yes, Diotima."

"And I will put the implant into Princess this morning."

"You, Diotima?"

"I don't want any mistakes, and when she comes out of anesthesia, I want you there to look after her."

"Yes, Diotima."

"I'm serious, Elliot. There will be no 'accidents' with Princess."

When Elliot bowed and left, Diotima crossed through the fortress to the hospital. Without looking in on the patient first, she put a sterile plastic bag over her head and washed up for the operation.

They were relatively safe in the snowy mountains above the city of Aspen. Homo Insectus hated the cold, and machines struggled on the sloping hills. They raised goats for milk, meat, and cheese, and supplemented their diet with small plots of vegetables. Through hard times and good, the little tribe survived, growing to as many as sixty people at one time.

Generations grew, got restless, and moved on to establish camps down in the valleys where risks were greater but the soil more fertile. Sometimes they heard back from these colonies but more often not.

Mindy was part of the next restless generation. In the small tribe of forty people at that time, there were no young men to marry who were not closely related. Four of her male cousins and two females in the same situation were planning to leave, either to join a camp in the valley or to find a mate to bring back up the hill.

They dressed in their best clothes bought from the traders who plundered empty cities. They filled their packs with dried goat strips and cheese. They kissed their families goodbye and set off along a crumbling asphalt road.

Halfway down the mountain they stopped at an abandoned Ranger's Station for lunch. They drank at the stream and stretched out around a cluster of picnic tables for a nap.

A low vibration shook the air, and a shadow raced across the ground. A silver machine hovered three hundred meters above them. It wasn't one of the small quiet planes that killed with silver stones, but a giant noisy machine that threatened to suck the air out of their lungs.

As the machine dropped, Mindy screamed and ran for the trees with the rest. When she chanced a look behind, metal spiders were scuttling out of the open door of the mothership. Such a great expenditure for biomass, Mindy thought as she ran. That factory would not last a season.

Mindy and her cousins were in among the trees but the carryalls didn't stop. They crashed through the underbrush herding the group together. On and on they ran until they had been surrounded. Dale shouted, "Up the trees!"

Mindy flung away her pack and launched herself for the lowest branches. Fighting through needles and sap that pulled at her long black hair. She stopped five meters above the ground, chest heaving as she tried to catch her breath. Sure enough, they were surrounded. From all sides of the forest, carryalls crawled towards them, angling cameras to examine their catch.

The seven of them were trapped, the three fastest boys in front of her, one boy and the two other girls behind her. Mindy could only see four of them from her tree but they yelled as the carryalls closed in.

Furthest out front, Roger yelled, "They passed me by. I'm going to run and see if they follow."

"Good luck," the others yelled and Roger was gone.

In the very back, Dora yelled, "One of them looked at me and walked by."

Mindy yelled, "Climb down and run away!"

Mindy's heart beat faster as the circle of carryalls tightened around her. They were looking for someone specific! The ones who climbed down and ran were safe. When Mindy stepped a branch lower, two carryalls buzzed to the foot of her tree. They cut at the lowest branches with spinning saws on their tool arms. Dale just ahead of her yelled, "It's you Mindy. They want you."

"Don't leave me!" she pleaded as Dale climbed down. The carryalls ignored him, and pressed tighter to her tree.

Dale screamed, "We'll always remember you, Mindy," and was gone.

At least the machines were too heavy to climb, and Mindy swore she would die of dehydration before climbing down. They cut and dragged away branches, as Mindy climbed into the highest supporting branches.

"Just go away!" she yelled, and then with a crack, her tree started to lean. The carryalls were ripping into the trunk. As the tree gained momentum, Mindy braced her feet. With no destination in sight she jumped for her life and banged her head. She felt her body impaled on pine as the world turned black.

Mindy woke in a bed softer than any she felt in her life. Her wounds stung under gauze bandages, but her body and the bed sheets were free of the normal grit. Other than the bed, the room was completely empty except for two doors. Dressed in a thin cotton nightgown she climbed out of bed finding a toilet and shower behind one door. The other door was locked. Mindy kicked and yelled, "Hey! Let me out!"

After a few minutes she gave up and pressed her ear to the door. Other than a continuous soft vibration she could hear nothing. A half hour later the door lock clicked. Mindy ran to the bathroom. She peered out as a carryall scuttled in with a tray of food. It set the tray on the floor while another stood guard in the empty hallway beyond.

Mindy ate corn and rice from the tray. She drank water from a jug, and because she had nothing else to do, she took a shower. The carryall returned an hour later for the tray. Mindy slept. She woke when the carryall returned with more food.

Hiding in the bathroom whenever the door clicked, Mindy was never bothered by the carryalls and she never bothered them. Once a week a new nightgown was brought with the tray. She left her old one to be carried away and that was her life.

It was impossible to tell how much time passed. The lights never dimmed. Meals seemed to be spaced out three per day, possibly mimicking the breakfast, lunch, and dinner of an outside reality. Mindy started saving a kernel of corn from each first-meal in order to count the days. She collected them behind the bed, but she got hungry one night and ate them all. What meaning had time anymore?

When the routine finally changed, it was not for the better. The two carryalls came but there was no food. They caught her with steel cuffs and dragged her into the hallway. She was pulled to another room and tied to a bed with restraints on her arms and legs.

When a nightmare creature strode in on flashing steel legs, Mindy fought to escape. With the grace of a dancer it approached the bed. A decapitated head on top was sealed in a plastic bag. Camera lenses poked out from the dead eyeballs looking down at her as she struggled. The nightmare creature did not say a word as it lowered a plastic rubber mask over her face. Mindy felt cold fingers on her chin and cheek as the world went black once more.

Mindy's eyes fluttered. She felt sick to her stomach and her head pounded. When she groaned and tried to roll to the side, gentle hands held her arms. For a second she thought it was the steel woman with a green ichorous head, but the hands were soft and warm. Surely that steel creature had only been a nightmare.

When Mindy's vision cleared, the man she saw was only slightly less frightening. A mass of blinking lights protruded from the right side of his head. He smiled at her. "My name is Elliot."

Mindy coughed and tried to throw up. "I feel sick."

Elliot held a wash cloth to her lips. "It's the anesthesia. Suck some water for your throat."

Mindy sucked the cloth dry and asked for more. Elliot dipped it in a bowl and gave it back. "Do you know where you are?"

Mindy shook her head.

"You are in a machine fortress. You were captured by machines like I was."

Mindy's eyes were drawn again to the blinking lights. "They did that to you?"

"It is a fibrous spindle that sends thousands of fibers through my cortex. When neuron bundles fire in my brain, these fibers record the pattern. From a library of recorded patterns, the machines can see roughly what I'm thinking."

"How horrible!"

"It's painless though, is it not?"

Mindy's eyes widened as understanding slowly dawned. She held a trembling hand to her head and screamed and screamed.